Whispers of the Willow:
The Chronicles of Finn and the Hidden Truth

I0614342

THE TORTOISE'S Timeless WISDOM

✴ ·········· Book Two ·········· ✴

Anthony Ofili Nwosisi

The Tortoise's Timeless Wisdom

Book 2 of The Chronicles of Finn and the Hidden Truth

Copyright © 2025 by Anthony Ofili Nwosisi

Published by Lucid Books in Houston, TX
www.LucidBooks.com

ISBN: 978-1-63296-881-4 (Paperback)
ISBN: 978-1-63296-882-1 (Hardback)
eISBN: 978-1-63296-885-2

Special Sales: Most Lucid Books titles are available in special quantity discounts. Custom imprinting or excerpting can also be done to fit special needs. Contact Lucid Books at Info@LucidBooks.com

Disclaimer

✦ ⋯⋯ Dedication ⋯⋯ ✦

To those who walk slowly,
not because the world waits for them,
but because they know each step is its own universe.

To the quiet souls who listen for the wisdom between heartbeats,
and to the patient dreamers who understand
that the truest answers arrive
only when time is ready to give them.

May this journey be your mirror,
and may you find, in its stillness,
the courage to wait, the strength to endure,
and the joy of seeing all things ripen in their season.

Whispers of the Willow
The Chronicles of Finn and the Hidden Truth

Whispers of the Willow: The Chronicles of Finn and the Hidden Truth unfolds across twelve books, each containing twelve stories that reflect the stages of Finn's journey. These books are not merely episodes of adventure; they are chapters in the profound journey of self-discovery, moral growth, and the realization of the importance of unity.

Books 1–4: The Awakening of Wisdom – In the first four books, Finn's journey begins with the realization of the darkness that threatens Everleaf. These books focus on the early stages of his intellectual and emotional awakening. Finn learns the value of patience from the tortoise, the difference between superficial knowledge and true wisdom from the crow, and the importance of inner peace from the silent stream. These lessons are foundational, laying the groundwork for the challenges he will face later.

Books 5–8: The Trials of Courage and Leadership – The middle section of the series delves into themes of courage, leadership, and moral integrity. Finn is tested by the riddle of the rustling leaves, which challenges his growing wisdom. He faces the whispering winds, where he must muster his courage in the face of fear. The guardian of the hidden grove teaches him about the responsibilities of leadership, while the serpent's silver tongue presents a trial of moral integrity, as Finn must discern truth from deception.

Books 9–12: The Revelation and Restoration – The final books bring Finn's journey to its climax and resolution. The dance of the fireflies symbolizes the unity that will be crucial to overcoming the darkness. The ancient owl's visions provide Finn with a broader understanding of his quest, showing him the interconnectedness of all life in Everleaf. In the veil of the vanishing mist, Finn confronts his deepest doubts and learns to see through the illusions that have clouded his mind. In the final book, Finn uncovers the source of the darkness within and leads the creatures of Everleaf in restoring balance to their world.

Impactful Themes: A Deeper Exploration

Wisdom vs. Knowledge

Throughout the series, the distinction between knowledge and wisdom is a central theme. But what is wisdom? In our modern world, wisdom is often conflated with knowledge, yet these are far from the same thing. Knowledge is information—facts, data, and experiences catalogued in the mind. But wisdom is the art of understanding how to apply that knowledge in service of a greater good. Wisdom is discernment, the ability to see past the surface of things and grasp a deeper essence of life. It is the awareness that life is not just a series of events but a complex web of meaning, responsibility, and choice. Wisdom is about living well, not just knowing much.

Finn's journey is not just about acquiring information but about learning how to apply it meaningfully. The tortoise's lesson in patience, the crow's challenge of superficial knowledge, and the riddle of the rustling leaves all underscore the importance of wisdom—of understanding the deeper truths that lie beneath the surface of facts.

Courage and Resilience

Finn's trials often involve facing fear and uncertainty, teaching young readers that true courage is not the absence of fear but the strength to confront it. The night of the whispering winds and the veil of the vanishing mist both serve as powerful metaphors for the inner struggles we all face and must overcome as a key part of growth.

Unity and Leadership

A recurring theme in the series is the power of unity and the responsibilities of leadership. Finn learns that leadership is not about dominance but about guiding others with wisdom, compassion, and integrity. The guardian of the hidden grove and the dance of the fireflies illustrate how collective strength and unity are vital to overcoming challenges, emphasizing that we are stronger together than alone.

The Heart of the Story

Whispers of the Willow: The Chronicles of Finn and the Hidden Truth is more than just a children's book series; it is a profound exploration of the human condition, told through the lens of a young fox's journey in a mystical forest. The series invites readers to reflect on the nature of wisdom, the importance of courage, and the power of unity. Each story is a stepping stone in Finn's journey, and by extension, in the journey of every reader who joins him on this adventure.

This series is designed to captivate young minds while offering deep moral and philosophical lessons that resonate with readers of all ages. It is a work of art that speaks to the heart, challenges the mind, and ultimately, leaves a lasting impression on the soul.

This is the story of Finn, but it is also the story of all of us, as we navigate the complexities of life, seeking wisdom, facing our fears, and discovering the unseen truths that lie within.

Looking Ahead: The Journey Continues

As Finn's journey progresses, the lessons of Books 1–4, The Awakening of Wisdom, serve as the foundation for the greater trials he will face. In the upcoming parts of the series, The Trials of Courage and Leadership and The Revelation and Restoration, Finn will be tested in ways that challenge his newfound wisdom. He will learn the true meaning of courage, the responsibilities of leadership, and the interconnectedness of all life in Everleaf. These lessons will culminate in a final confrontation with the darkness that threatens his world—a confrontation that will require every ounce of wisdom, strength, and peace that Finn has gained.

So, as you finish this first part of Finn's journey, I invite you to reflect on the lessons of wisdom that have been woven into these chronicles. These are not just Finn's lessons; they are yours as well. Carry them with you as you continue to explore the world and know that the journey of wisdom is a lifelong endeavor, one that will guide you through every challenge you face.

And as you look forward to the volumes of Finn's journey, know that the best is yet to come. The trials ahead will be difficult, but with wisdom as your guide, you will be prepared to face them, just as Finn is.

A Guide to the Journey Continues

With the first book now in the hands of readers, the path through Everleaf grows deeper, richer, and more personal. "The Tortoise's Timeless Wisdom" marks not just a continuation but a turning. The forest begins to speak in slower tones, and time itself becomes a companion rather than a cage.

This second book calls upon the reader to walk differently—to feel, pause, and listen with the heart as much as the mind. Here, Finn learns that wisdom is not a destination but a rhythm. That presence is not merely being there but being aware. And that sometimes, what changes us most are the things that appear still.

As the series unfolds across twelve books, each story remains a whisper in the greater chorus—a reminder that knowledge is not rushed, and truth reveals itself only when we are ready to see it.

Welcome to the next step.

Book	Book Title	Thematic Focus
1	The Shadow Beneath the Leaves	Introduces the creeping darkness in Everleaf and Finn's initial realization that something is amiss. Sets the stage for the quest and establishes the overarching conflict.
2	The Tortoise's Timeless Wisdom	Finn's first encounter with wisdom and patience. He learns that understanding cannot be rushed, and that true knowledge comes with time and reflection.
3	The Crow's Tempting Knowledge	Explores the theme of discerning true wisdom from superficial knowledge. Finn faces a trial where he must choose between the allure of easy answers and the depth of true understanding.
4	The Song of the Silent Stream	Finn learns the importance of inner peace and listening to the quiet truths of the heart. The stream teaches him that sometimes, silence speaks louder than words.
5	The Riddle of the Rustling Leaves	A mysterious and challenging riddle tests Finn's growing wisdom. He learns that not all answers are straightforward, and that some truths must be felt, not just known.
6	The Night of the Whispering Winds	Finn faces a test of courage during a tumultuous night. He learns that resilience and bravery are found not in the absence of fear but in facing it head-on.
7	The Guardian of the Hidden Grove	A protector figure helps Finn understand the responsibility that comes with wisdom and leadership. He learns that being a guardian is not about power but about care and protection.
8	The Serpent's Silver Tongue	Finn confronts deceit and learns the critical lesson of trusting his instincts over persuasive but misleading appearances. The serpent represents the dangers of eloquence without substance.
9	The Dance of the Fireflies	A lighter episode where Finn discovers the beauty of unity and collaboration. The fireflies symbolize how individual strengths can create something magical when combined.
10	The Vision of the Ancient Owl	Guided by an owl, Finn receives visions of the past and future. He begins to see the bigger picture of his quest and understands the interconnectedness of all life in Everleaf.
11	The Veil of the Vanishing Mist	Finn faces the final test of self-doubt and uncertainty. The mist represents the illusions and doubts that cloud his mind, which he must see through to find the truth.
12	The Unseen Truth	The culmination of Finn's journey. He uncovers the ultimate truth about the darkness, which lies within, and through unity, he restores the balance of Everleaf.

The Sacred Mirror
Why Book 2 Matters

The Chronicles of Finn and the Hidden Truth Book 2 ⊠ The Tortoise's Timeless Wisdom

Book 2 is not a sequel. It is a threshold. A soul-deep pivot from wonder to wisdom.

Where Book 1 unfurled the mysteries of the cosmos through the eyes of innocent awe, Book 2 invites the reader to turn inward into the sacred stillness from which authentic transformation emerges.

This is not merely a continuation of the tale. It is a rite of passage. The forest still breathes. The winds still whisper. But something has shifted.

Finn is no longer merely observing. He is undergoing: A Becoming. And with him, so are you.

The Tortoise's Timeless Wisdom is not a map. It is a mirror. It does not tell you where to go. It reveals who you are.

Six Eternal Truths Beneath the Shell

These are not mere lessons or allegories. They are living, breathing truths: encoded in stillness, embedded in symbol, and rooted in soul. They do not shout. They do not rush. They unfold with reverence. The tortoise does not hurry. And neither does truth.

1. The Evolution of Wisdom

In an age where information overwhelms and comprehension withers, this book reclaims a forgotten axiom: Wisdom is not gathered. It is earned.

Not through acceleration, but through stillness. Not through certainty, but through surrender. Not through answers, but through silence.

Wisdom is not a possession; it is a posture. It is forged in failure, shaped by restraint, and disclosed only to those willing to wait.

This is not a book that instructs. It is a book that remembers. And in remembering, it reawakens something ancient within you.

2. Stillness as Sacred Preparation

Stillness is not passivity; it is potency veiled in patience. While the world clamours for attention, Book 2 dares to whisper. It invites you to detox from the addiction to speed, to unlearn the lie that waiting is weakness.

In the slowness of the tortoise, a deeper rhythm emerges —One that honours gestation, reveres silence, and magnifies presence.

If you find yourself suspended in uncertainty, stalled in direction, or estranged from clarity, this book will not push you forward. It will sanctify your pause. It will anoint your stillness. It will declare delay not as deficiency, but as divine design.

You are not behind. You are being refined.

3. Time as a Living Force

Time, in this world, is not linear. It is not mechanical, not a metric to be mastered. It is sacred.

The Rune of Time — etched into the tortoise's path and the forest's breath — discloses an ancient truth: Time bends for the attentive. It stretches for the present. It serves the sincere.

The past is not lost. The future is not fixed. Time becomes a spiralling current you enter with reverence.

You do not pass through time. Time passes through you.

4. The Sacred Ache of Becoming

Becoming is not soft. It is sacred. It bruises, it exposes, it reshapes.

To grow is to grieve. To transform is to ache. Not because pain is punishment, but because it is proof that something within you is shedding its illusion.

Finn does not vanquish his pain. He carries it with reverence. He walks through the shadows, not around them. And so must we.

This book does not rescue you from the storm. It sits with you inside it, and whispers:

"You are not broken. You are breaking open."

5. Destiny, Calling, and the Quiet Summons

In Book 1, Finn wandered. In Book 2, he begins to listen.

Not to thunder but to echo. Not to command but to presence.

The tortoise does not impose. It reveals. There is a chasm between chasing a destiny and becoming one who can carry it.

This is a book about sacred readiness.

You were not designed for noise. You were crafted for alignment.

This book does not ask you to rise with might. It invites you to descend with purpose into your truest self.

"Not all who wander are called," the forest murmurs. "But you, Finn, are being summoned…"

6. Identity as a Fluid Flame

Who you were is not who you must remain. Identity is not static; it is a sanctified flame.

It burns away what is performative, and reveals what is eternal.

Finn is not evolving through rebellion, but through revelation. From fox to bearer. From seeker to steward.

The tortoise does not teach him who to be. It teaches him how to listen for the soul that is becoming.

You are not obligated to remain who you were, even if others insist upon it. You are permitted to evolve. You are allowed to transcend.

This book grants you that permission and calls it sacred.

What This Book Will Do to You (If You Let It)

The Tortoise's Timeless Wisdom will not entertain. It will initiate.

If Book 1 cracked the shell of illusion, Book 2 brings you into the sacred soil of selfhood.

This is not for the hurried reader. It is for the seeker who:

Feels suspended in transition.

Hungers for deeper meaning.

Longs to live gently but truthfully.

Is weary of noise and hollow answers.

Is ready to awaken ancient truths buried within

This is not a tale. It is a turning. A sacred moment dressed in pages.

Final Invocation

The Tortoise's Timeless Wisdom does not explain your life. It reflects it.

It does not promise clarity. It promises companionship.

It does not offer escape. It offers elevation.

It gives you permission:

To grow slowly

To feel deeply

To live wisely

To become fully

You do not simply read this book. You Walk with it. And somewhere along the path, you awaken to this revelation: You are not who you were when you began.

The Spiral Path of Wisdom
A Prelude to the Inner Journey

Wisdom is not a summit to be scaled. It is a spiral path; a sacred unfolding through which one circles the same questions at deeper levels of understanding. The journey does not progress in straight lines, nor does it repeat itself. Rather, it invites us back — again and again — to familiar truths, each time with new eyes and a changed heart.

The tortoise, ancient and deliberate, does not sprint toward answers. It communes with the soil. It listens to the silence between seasons. It teaches us that depth, not distance, is the measure of growth.

The Spiral Begins Where the Circle Ends

In Book 1, we wandered in wonder with eyes wide open to the splendour and mystery of the world. In Book 2, the gaze turns inward. We begin to descend into ourselves, shedding the skin of spectacle in search of substance. The circle of curiosity matures into the spiral of contemplation.

Here, the old questions return:

Who am I, apart from expectation?

What matters when the applause fades?

Where does my path begin when no one is watching?

These are not new inquiries. But they echo differently in the chambers of the soul that has known silence.

Sacred Delays and Divine Detours

The spiral is patient. It does not conform to the clock of culture. It bends time toward transformation.

You may feel stalled. Forgotten. Misaligned.

But the spiral whispers: You are not behind. You are being deepened.

This is not punishment. It is preparation. Just as seeds split before they sprout, so too must we break before we blossom.

Every delay in this sacred journey is a divine detour not away from destiny, but toward the depth required to hold it.

Becoming Is Not Linear

To grow is not to ascend a ladder. It is to circle the same mountain, arriving each time not at the same place, but at the same truth — re-understood, re-embodied, re-lived.

The spiral reveals:

That wisdom cannot be inherited; it must be excavated.

That maturity is not the absence of struggle but the integration of it.

That progress is not speed but presence in the process.

The tortoise teaches not in lessons, but in rhythm. And the rhythm of transformation is not a march. It is a sacred dance with time.

The Forest as Mirror, the Tortoise as Guide

The forest no longer merely enchants. It reflects. Each rustling leaf, each shifting wind, speaks not only of mystery, but of memory of truths buried beneath your busyness.

The tortoise appears not to dazzle, but to disarm. It is the antithesis of the world's chaos. In its slowness, it reclaims tempo from tyranny. It leads by not leading. It invites by simply being.

This is the paradox of the spiral:

You go inward to find outward direction.

You slow down to move forward.

You return to begin anew.

The Spiral Awakens What the Ladder Cannot

The ladder asks, "How high can you climb?" The spiral asks, "How deep can you dwell?"

The ladder is built by ego. The spiral is carved by soul.

This book—The Tortoise's Timeless Wisdom—does not promise to lift you higher. It promises to take you deeper. Into truth. Into self. Into resonance with the sacred tempo of your becoming.

Final Orientation: A Journey That Turns You into Itself

This is not a book to rush through. It is a path to be walked with reverence.

Let the spiral path reorient your mind, your rhythm, and your reason for the journey.

You are not lost. You are being led inward. You are not stuck. You are circling deeper. You are not who you were. You are who you are becoming.

Walk slowly. Walk truly. Walk as one who remembers the way home.

The Cost of Becoming
A Practical Reflection

Imagine a young professional — brilliant, driven, and adorned with accolades since childhood. Their every step is applauded, every success affirmed. They pursue excellence with relentless precision: more goals, more recognition, more momentum. And yet, beneath this polished trajectory lies a quiet erosion — a soul quietly fraying at the edges.

Each morning greets them not with purpose, but with pressure. Their calendar is full, yet their heart is hollow. The performance continues — composed smiles, eloquent presentations, strategic deliverables — but in the silence between meetings, a whisper persists:

"Why does none of this feel like enough?"

Then, in a rare moment of stillness — when exhaustion has finally silenced ambition — they encounter Finn's story. And something elemental begins to shift.

For the first time, they glimpse the possibility that **becoming** is not a conquest, but a return. Not a sprint, but a sacred unfolding. They do not slow down because they are burnt out. They slow down because they are awakening.

They begin to see that the essence of transformation is not performance, but presence.

They no longer seek success for applause, but alignment. No longer chase validation, but voice. No longer climb ladders, but descend into truth.

They begin listening — truly listening — not to the noise of the world, but to the echo within. They make fewer moves, but each is weighted with intention. They stop speaking to be heard and begin speaking from what matters. Their yes becomes discerning. Their no becomes sacred.

They realise, with sobering clarity, that true greatness is not measured by volume, but by **vocation**. That fulfilment cannot be replicated, outsourced, or purchased. It must be lived — authentically, slowly, deeply — and it must be earned through courage, contemplation, and sacrifice.

In this inner reorientation, their external world realigns. They are no longer defined by systems or titles, but by **substance**. They do not belong to institutions or paradigms, but to their path. To truth. To purpose.

This is the cost of becoming:

To release applause in order to hold truth. To disappoint expectations in order to honour identity. To walk alone in order to walk honestly.

But the reward is immeasurable: A life no longer dictated by performance, But illumined by presence. A life anchored in meaning, Directed by purpose, And quietly aflame with inner light.

THE
TORTOISE'S
Timeless
WISDOM

The Ever-Present Whisper

I n the heart of Everleaf, where the ancient trees stood tall and proud, their roots entwined in the rich, fertile soil of time itself, there was a silence that was anything but empty. It was a silence filled with the whispers of the past, the murmurs of wisdom passed down through the ages, and the echoes of the many lives that had come and gone beneath the boughs of the Great Willow. This silence, though profound, was not a void; it was the breath of the forest, a living, breathing testament to the patience and persistence that had shaped it over millennia.

As dawn approached, the first light of day began to filter through the dense canopy, casting long, golden beams across the forest floor. The air was cool, with a hint of dew still clinging to the leaves, and the scent of earth and wood filled the space between the trees. It was a time of transition,

a moment when the world seemed to be suspended between the darkness of night and the brightness of day. And at that moment, the Great Willow began to whisper.

The whisper was soft, almost imperceptible, yet it carried with it the weight of countless years, the knowledge of a thousand lifetimes. It was a voice that spoke not to the ears but to the heart, to the soul, to the very essence of what it meant to be alive in this ancient, mystical place. It was a voice that had guided countless creatures on their journeys, offering wisdom, comfort, and most of all, patience.

"Time," the Great Willow whispered, "is not a river to be rushed, nor a burden to be borne. Time is the soil from which all things grow. It is the bedrock of understanding, the foundation upon which wisdom is built. To truly know the world, one must first know time, not as a fleeting moment but as an ever-present companion, a constant, silent guide."

Finn, the young fox who had once raced through the forest with the urgency of one who believes time is running out, stood beneath the Great Willow, his heart open to the whispers that swirled around him. He had come far from the beginning of his journey; he had faced the shadow that crept through Everleaf and confronted the fears within his own heart. Yet, despite all he had accomplished, Finn knew that his journey had only just begun.

Prologue

The Great Willow's words were a balm to Finn's soul, a reminder that not all progress was made in leaps and bounds, that sometimes the most important lessons were learned not through action but through stillness; through observation; through the quiet, patient understanding that time alone could bring. The urgency that had once driven him now seemed a distant memory, replaced by a sense of calm, purpose, and a deeper, more profound understanding of the world around him.

"Your path," the Great Willow continued, "is one of patience, of wisdom, of learning to see the world not as it is but as it has always been and as it will always be. The shadows you face are not merely the absence of light but the absence of understanding and connection to the world and time itself. To dispel them, you must first learn to listen to the whispers of the wind, to the song of the earth, and to the voice of time that speaks through every living thing."

Finn closed his eyes, letting the whispers wash over him, feeling them seep into his very being. He understood now that his journey would require more than courage, more than strength. It would require patience—the kind of patience that Griselda, the wise tortoise, had shown him in their brief encounters. Griselda moved with a slowness that belied her wisdom, a deliberate pace that allowed her to see and understand things that others, in

their haste, would miss. Finn knew that she would be his guide in the days to come and that she would teach him the ways of time, of patience, of wisdom.

The forest around him was waking slowly, the creatures of Everleaf stirring in their nests, their burrows, their hidden places. But there was no rush, no urgency. The world moved at its own pace, a rhythm set by the Great Willow, by the ancient trees that had stood for centuries, their roots deep in the earth, their branches high in the sky. It was a rhythm that Finn was beginning to understand, to feel in his own heart and soul.

As he opened his eyes and looked up at the Great Willow, Finn felt a sense of peace settle over him, a calmness that was beginning to feel familiar. The journey ahead would be long, the path uncertain, but he was ready to learn, to grow, to embrace the wisdom that time had to offer. The Great Willow's whispers were with him, guiding him, reminding him that the answers he sought would not come quickly but would reveal themselves in time, if only he had the patience to wait, to listen, to understand.

"Remember," the Great Willow whispered, "wisdom is not found in haste but in stillness. It is not a prize to be won but a gift to be received, a gift that time alone can give. Trust in time; trust in the journey, and you will find what you seek."

Prologue

With those final words echoing in his mind, Finn turned away from the Great Willow and began to walk, his steps slow and deliberate, his heart open to the journey ahead. He knew that he would face many challenges, that the shadows still lurked in the corners of Everleaf, waiting for the moment to strike. But he also knew that he was not the same fox who had begun this journey. He was wiser now, more patient, more attuned to the world around him.

And as he walked, Finn felt the presence of Griselda growing stronger, her wisdom and patience, guiding him through the forest. She would be his mentor and guide, the one who would teach him the timeless wisdom of the tortoise, the ancient knowledge that had been passed down through the ages. It was knowledge that Finn knew he needed, wisdom that would help him face the challenges ahead, and patience that would carry him through the darkest of times.

The prologue to Finn's new journey had been written, the stage set for the lessons to come. And as the first light of day broke through the canopy, casting a soft, golden glow across the forest, Finn knew that he was ready to embrace the wisdom of time, to learn the lessons that would shape his future, to walk the path of patience and understanding that the Great Willow had laid before him.

The Tortoise's Timeless Wisdom

Finn was no longer afraid. He would face whatever came next with the whispers of the Great Willow in his heart, the wisdom of Griselda in his mind, and the patience of time as his guide.

Chapter 1
The Slow Path Forward

The sun had just begun its ascent, casting long shadows across the forest floor, where the dew still clung to the leaves like tiny jewels. Finn stood at the edge of a path that was barely discernible beneath the dense undergrowth. It was as though the forest itself had forgotten this place, allowing time to weave its threads, undisturbed and unnoticed, into the fabric of the earth. The air was thick, almost heavy, with a stillness that pressed down on him, urging him to proceed with caution. Every instinct within him whispered that this was not a place to be rushed—that here, in this forgotten corner of Everleaf, haste would be met with resistance.

Finn took a deep breath, filling his lungs with the scent of damp earth and decaying leaves. The forest around him

seemed to hum with an ancient energy, a rhythm that was slow and deliberate, far removed from the urgency he had felt during the earlier parts of his journey. The path ahead was narrow, winding through trees that towered above him, their branches intertwined to form a canopy so thick that it allowed only the faintest traces of light to filter through. It was as if time itself had slowed here, each moment stretching out like a long shadow, leaving Finn with the unsettling sensation that he was moving through a world apart from the one he had known.

The first few steps were tentative, almost hesitant, as Finn tried to adjust to the unfamiliar pace. The ground beneath his paws was uneven, littered with fallen branches and the tangled roots of ancient trees that seemed to reach up from the earth like the gnarled fingers of some unseen giant. Every movement required careful consideration, every step a deliberate act of will. The urgency that had once driven him so fiercely now felt out of place as if it would disturb the delicate balance of this hidden part of the forest.

As he ventured deeper, the path grew narrower, the underbrush thicker, until it was no longer clear where the trail ended, and the forest began. Finn's progress slowed to a crawl, his sharp eyes scanning the ground ahead for any sign of the way forward. But the forest offered no clear direction, no obvious markers to guide him. Instead, it seemed to whisper a silent challenge: To move forward, Finn would need to slow down to match the rhythm of this place and become a part of the forest rather than an intruder upon it.

The Slow Path Forward

The discomfort was immediate and acute. Finn had always been quick, agile, his movements driven by a keen mind that thrived on action and discovery. But here, in this dense, slow-moving part of Everleaf, those qualities seemed more hindrance than help. His natural urge to push forward to find the next clue, the next challenge, was met with resistance at every turn. The forest seemed to resist his every move, forcing him to slow down, to take stock, to truly see what was around him.

And what he saw were the subtle signs of a presence far older and wiser than his own. The first of these signs was a worn path, almost invisible beneath the thick carpet of leaves, yet unmistakably there, a faint trail that wound its way through the trees like a thread through a tapestry. It was a path that had been walked many times, not by the hurried feet of those who sought to conquer the forest but by the slow, deliberate steps of one who understood its secrets.

Finn's heart quickened as he realized what this meant. These were Griselda's paths, the trails left behind by the wise tortoise who had moved through this forest with a patience and understanding that Finn could only aspire to. The realization was both comforting and humbling, a reminder that he was not alone on this journey, that others had walked this path before him, leaving behind the faintest traces of their wisdom for those who were willing to see.

He followed the path carefully, each step a conscious decision, each movement slow and deliberate. The farther he went, the more signs he found: ancient markings carved into the trunks of trees, small piles of stones that had been

carefully arranged, the faintest trace of a scent that was familiar and comforting. These were Griselda's markers, the signs of her presence, her wisdom, her understanding of the forest. They were there to guide him but only if he was willing to slow down, to see them, to truly appreciate the knowledge they held.

But slowing down was not easy. Finn could feel impatience bubbling just beneath the surface, a restless energy that urged him to move faster, to push forward, to find the answers he sought. It was an urge that had served him well in the past and had driven him to confront the darkness that threatened Everleaf. But here, in this part of the forest, that same urgency felt out of place, almost dangerous. It was as if the forest itself was testing him, challenging him to let go of his need for speed and action and to embrace a different way of moving through the world.

The struggle was internal as much as it was external. Finn could feel the tension in his muscles, the impatience in his thoughts, the frustration that came from moving so slowly when every instinct screamed at him to go faster. But he knew, deep down, that this was a lesson he needed to learn, that the forest was offering him something far more valuable than speed or strength. It was offering him wisdom, the kind of wisdom that could only be gained through patience; stillness; and the deliberate, careful observation of the world around him.

As the day wore on, Finn began to notice changes in himself. The tension in his body slowly began to ease, the restlessness in his mind giving way to a quiet, almost

meditative state. The path ahead was no longer a challenge to be overcome but a journey to be experienced. Each step was a moment of connection with the forest—each movement an opportunity to learn, to grow, to understand.

And with that understanding came a deeper appreciation for the world around him. The forest was no longer just a place to be explored; it was a living, breathing entity with its own rhythms, its own pace, its own wisdom. The trees, the earth, the very air seemed to pulse with a slow, deliberate energy that Finn could feel in his bones, a rhythm that he was beginning to match with his own movements and thoughts.

The discomfort that had plagued him at the beginning of his journey was fading, replaced by a sense of peace and connection. Finn could feel the presence of Griselda all around him, guiding him, teaching him through the subtle signs she had left behind. It was a presence that was both comforting and challenging, a reminder that he still had much to learn, but also that he was on the right path.

As the sun began to set, casting long shadows across the forest floor, Finn came to a small clearing. The air was warm, filled with the scent of wildflowers and the soft hum of insects. It was a peaceful place that invited stillness and reflection. And as Finn stood there, feeling the last rays of the sun on his fur, he realized that he had begun to learn the lesson the forest had been trying to teach him all along.

The slow path forward was not a burden, not a challenge to be overcome but a gift. It was an opportunity to see

the world in a new way, to understand the deep, ancient wisdom that time and patience could offer. It was a lesson that Finn knew he would carry with him, a lesson that would shape his journey in ways he could not yet fully understand.

And as the first stars began to appear in the sky, Finn lay down in the soft grass, his heart filled with quiet, peaceful contentment. The path ahead was still long, the challenges still great, but he was ready to move forward, slowly, deliberately, with the wisdom of the forest as his guide.

The Meeting with Griselda

The sun was climbing higher into the sky, its rays filtering through the dense canopy, casting dappled patterns of light and shadow on the forest floor. Finn, having navigated the slow and deliberate path that seemed to wind endlessly through the thickest parts of Everleaf, found himself in a small, serene clearing. The air here was still, almost reverent, as if the very forest was holding its breath in anticipation of what was to come. The ground was covered in soft moss, and the ancient trees that surrounded the clearing stood tall and silent, their roots twisted and knotted like the veins of the earth itself.

Finn's steps were cautious as he entered this sacred space, his senses heightened by the quietude that seemed to hum with the weight of countless years. There was a presence

here, something old and wise, something that had seen the rise and fall of generations, that had witnessed the turning of countless seasons. It was as if time itself had taken residence in this place, moving not in the rapid pulse of seconds and minutes but in the slow, deliberate rhythm of centuries.

And then, from the far side of the clearing, Finn saw her.

Griselda the tortoise was unlike any creature Finn had encountered before. She was ancient, her shell a mosaic of patterns etched deep by the passage of time, each groove and ridge telling a story of a life lived in harmony with the forest. Her eyes, dark and knowing, held a depth that seemed to reach back to the very beginnings of Everleaf. She moved with a grace that belied her age, each step slow, deliberate, yet with a certainty that spoke of an intimate understanding of the world around her.

Finn watched, mesmerized, as Griselda made her way toward him, her movements unhurried, her gaze never wavering. There was no rush in her, no urgency, just a quiet confidence, as if she knew that all things would come in their own time, that there was no need to force the world to move at a faster pace. The forest seemed to respond to her presence, the trees leaning slightly closer, the air growing warmer, more inviting as if the very earth was welcoming her.

"Finn," Griselda's voice was soft, yet it carried with it the weight of ages, a voice that seemed to come not just from the tortoise before him but from the very heart of the forest

itself. "You have come far, young one, but your journey has only just begun."

Finn bowed his head slightly, not out of fear or subservience but out of respect for the wisdom that radiated from Griselda. He could feel the tension in his body ease as her presence washed over him, a calm settling in his mind as he realized that here, in this place, there was no need to hurry, no need to push forward with the urgency that had driven him for so long.

"Why does everything feel so slow here?" Finn asked, his voice barely above a whisper, as if he feared that speaking too loudly would shatter the delicate stillness of the clearing.

Griselda paused, her gaze softening as she regarded him. "Because, Finn, time moves differently in places where it is understood, where it is honored," she replied. "Here, in this part of the forest, time is not something to be measured or chased. It is something to be experienced, to be lived fully. It is in the stillness, in the quiet moments that you truly come to understand the world, and yourself."

Finn frowned slightly, his mind grappling with the concept. "But . . . how can we learn, how can we grow, if we don't keep moving forward? If we don't keep pushing?"

Griselda smiled, a slow, deliberate movement that seemed to carry the warmth of the sun itself. "Ah, but that is where you must learn the difference between movement and progress, between haste and wisdom. Moving forward does not always mean rushing ahead. Sometimes, the greatest growth happens when you stand still, when you take the

time to observe, to reflect, to let the world reveal itself to you in its own time."

She turned slightly, her gaze sweeping across the clearing. "Look around you, Finn. What do you see?"

Finn followed her gaze, taking in the clearing, the trees, the soft light filtering through the leaves. "I see . . . the forest, the trees, the light, the moss on the ground."

Griselda nodded. "Yes, but look closer. What do you really see?"

Finn furrowed his brow, focusing his attention on the details he had overlooked. The trees were not just trees; they were ancient sentinels, their bark worn smoothly in places by the passage of countless creatures. The light was not just light; it was the sun's way of touching the earth, of nourishing the plants that grew in the shadows. The moss on the ground was not just a carpet of green; it was a living organism, thriving in the cool dampness, a testament to the persistence of life in even the most hidden corners of the world.

"I see... life," Finn whispered, the realization dawning on him. "I see how everything is connected, how everything moves together, even when it seems like nothing is moving at all."

Griselda's smile deepened. "Yes, Finn. That is the wisdom of time. It is in the stillness that you begin to see the connections, the patterns, the rhythms of the world. It is in the quiet moments that the forest reveals its secrets, not

through noise or haste but through patience, through the slow unfolding of life."

Finn felt a warmth spread through him, a sense of peace that he had not known before. The forest, which had once seemed like a vast and unknowable place, now felt like a living, breathing entity, one that he was a part of, one that he could learn from if he only took the time to listen, to observe.

Griselda began to move again, her slow, deliberate steps drawing Finn's attention back to her. "Come," she said, her voice gentle but firm. "There is much for you to learn, but you must first learn to be still, to let the world come to you, rather than trying to force your way through it."

Finn followed her, his steps matching her pace, the impatience that had once driven him now tempered by a newfound understanding. As they walked, Griselda began to speak, her voice weaving stories of the forest, of the creatures that lived within it, of the cycles of life and death, growth, and decay, that had shaped Everleaf over the millennia.

She spoke of the ancient trees, their roots deep in the earth, their branches reaching for the sky, each one a bridge between the past and the future. She told of the rivers that had carved their way through the land, slowly, over countless years, shaping the valleys and the hills, creating the very landscape that Finn now walked upon. She shared the wisdom of the stars, distant and cold, yet constant, their light a reminder that time is not something to be feared but something to be embraced.

The Tortoise's Timeless Wisdom

Finn listened, his mind absorbing the stories, the lessons, the wisdom that Griselda offered. Each word, each story was a piece of the puzzle, a thread in the tapestry of understanding that was slowly beginning to take shape within him. The impatience that had once been his constant companion was fading, replaced by a sense of wonder, curiosity, and an abiding respect for the world around him.

They walked for what felt like hours, though Finn could not say for certain. Time seemed to lose its meaning, slipping away like water through his paws, leaving only the present moment—the now, the here. And in that moment, Finn realized that he had begun to see the world in a new way, not as a place to be conquered or rushed through but as a place to be experienced, to be lived fully, with patience, understanding, and wisdom.

As they reached the edge of the clearing, Griselda stopped, turning to face Finn. "Remember this, Finn," she said, her voice soft, yet filled with the weight of the truth. "Wisdom is not something you can chase, or force, or rush. It is something that comes to you in its own time when you are ready to receive it. And that readiness comes not from moving quickly but from being still, from observing, from allowing yourself to be a part of the world, rather than just passing through it."

Finn nodded, the words sinking deep into his heart, into his soul. He knew that he still had much to learn, that the path ahead would not be easy, but he also knew that he was ready to embrace the slow, deliberate pace of wisdom—ready to let the forest and Griselda guide him on this journey.

The Meeting with Griselda

As they parted ways, Finn felt a sense of calm settle over him, a calm that came from knowing that he was moving at exactly the pace he needed to move. The forest was his teacher, time his guide, and Griselda his mentor. And with that knowledge, Finn took his first steps on the path of wisdom, a path that would lead him to unimaginable places; to lessons he had never dreamed of; to a future shaped not by haste but by patience, understanding, and the timeless wisdom of the forest.

Lessons of the Earth

The morning air was thick with the scent of damp soil and decaying leaves as Finn followed Griselda deeper into the heart of Everleaf. The trees around them seemed to be taller and older the farther they went; their bark was rough and knotted, and their roots were twisting and curling like ancient serpents through the earth. This was a part of the forest that felt different from anywhere Finn had been before. It felt quieter, heavier as if the very ground beneath his paws carried the weight of countless centuries.

Griselda moved slowly, her every step deliberate, her ancient eyes scanning the surroundings with a knowing gaze. Finn could feel the earth beneath him, solid and unyielding, yet alive with a subtle energy that he had never noticed before.

The Tortoise's Timeless Wisdom

It was as if the ground itself was whispering secrets, ancient truths buried deep within the layers of soil and stone, waiting to be uncovered by those patient enough to listen.

"Today, Finn," Griselda began, her voice a low, resonant hum that seemed to blend with the rustling of the leaves and the distant calls of the forest creatures, "we delve into the very essence of this world, into the earth itself. For it is in the soil, in the roots, in the deep, dark places where light rarely touches, that true wisdom lies hidden. Wisdom that has been nurtured and grown over millennia, waiting for those who seek it with patience and humility."

Finn nodded, though he was not entirely sure what Griselda meant. His journey so far had been one of discovery, of uncovering the mysteries of the forest, but this felt different, more profound, more connected to the very fabric of the world around him. He could sense the importance of what was to come, and though he didn't fully understand it, he felt a deep desire to learn, to grasp the lessons that Griselda was about to impart.

As they walked, Griselda led Finn to a small clearing where the ground was soft and rich, the soil dark and fertile, teeming with life. The clearing was surrounded by ancient trees, their roots exposed in places, winding through the earth like veins, each one telling the story of centuries of growth. Finn crouched down, his paws sinking slightly into the soft earth, feeling the cool, moist soil between his claws.

Lessons of the Earth

"Look at the ground beneath you, Finn," Griselda instructed, her voice calm and steady. "What do you see?"

Finn looked down, his sharp eyes scanning the surface of the soil. "I see the earth," he

replied, somewhat uncertainly. "The dirt, the roots of the trees, the fallen leaves," he added.

Griselda nodded slowly. "Yes, but what lies beneath? What stories does this earth hold, hidden from the eyes of those who do not take the time to dig deeper, to understand?"

Finn frowned, focusing his attention on the ground, trying to see beyond the surface. As he dug his claws into the soil, he began to uncover layers—small stones, fragments of old leaves, tiny insects scurrying away from the disturbance. But there was more, something deeper, something older.

Griselda watched him, her gaze patient and knowing. "The earth beneath us, Finn, is like the pages of a book, each layer a chapter in the history of this world. The roots you see are not just the physical support of the trees; they are the conduits of life, of knowledge, drawing sustenance from the past, from the memories buried deep within the soil. The fossils you find are remnants of lives long gone, but their essence—their wisdom—remains, passed down through the generations."

Finn paused, his mind slowly wrapping around the concept. He could see it now: The soil was a living record, each layer a testament to the passage of time and the countless lives that had come and gone, each one leaving behind a trace,

a memory, a lesson. The roots of the trees were the "veins" of the forest, carrying the lifeblood of the past into the present, connecting all that lived in Everleaf to the ancient wisdom that lay hidden in the earth.

"It's . . . it's like the forest itself is alive," Finn said softly, his voice filled with awe. "Not just the trees and the animals but everything—the soil, the roots, even the stones. They're all connected, all part of the same life, the same history."

Griselda's eyes gleamed with approval. "Yes, Finn. The forest is not just a collection of individual beings but a single, interconnected entity. Everything here, from the tallest tree to the smallest grain of sand, is part of a greater whole. And the earth beneath us is the foundation, the keeper of the stories, the guardian of the wisdom that has been passed down through time."

Finn sat back on his haunches, his mind spinning with the enormity of it all. He had always seen the forest as a place of mystery and adventure, a place to explore and conquer. But now, he understood that it was so much more—it was a living, breathing organism, a tapestry of life woven together by the threads of time and memory. And he was just a small part of it, one thread in a vast and ancient fabric that stretched back through the ages.

Griselda moved closer, her old, wise eyes meeting Finn's. "Humility, Finn," she said gently. "That is one of the greatest lessons the earth can teach us. We are not the masters of this world but its caretakers, its students. To truly learn, to truly grow in wisdom, we must first understand our place

within the greater whole. We must recognize that we are but a small part of something much larger, something that has existed long before us and will continue long after we are gone."

Finn nodded, the weight of Griselda's words settling over him like a blanket. He had always been so focused on his own journey, on his own quest for knowledge and understanding, that he had forgotten to look at the bigger picture, to see himself as part of the greater whole. It was a humbling realization but also a comforting one. For in recognizing his smallness, his place within the grand design of the forest, Finn felt a deeper connection to the world around him, a connection that transcended his individual existence.

Griselda began to dig into the soil with her strong, clawed feet, turning over the earth to reveal deeper layers. "Come, Finn," she instructed. "Let us explore the stories buried within the earth. Let us uncover the wisdom that lies hidden beneath the surface, waiting for those with the patience and humility to find it."

Finn joined her, his paws working alongside hers as they dug into the rich soil. They uncovered roots that were thick and gnarled, winding their way through the earth like the tendrils of some ancient creature. They found stones that were smooth and worn, shaped by the passage of countless years, each one a testament to the relentless march of time. And deeper still, they found the remnants of creatures long gone—fossils of bones, shells, and leaves, each one a fragment of a life that had once been part of the forest.

The Tortoise's Timeless Wisdom

As they dug, Griselda shared stories of the forest's past, of the creatures that had lived and died, their wisdom and knowledge passed down through the earth, through the very fabric of the forest itself. She spoke of the cycles of life and death, of growth and decay, and how each generation built upon the wisdom of those that had come before, adding to the tapestry of life that made up Everleaf.

Finn listened; his heart filled with a sense of reverence and awe. He could see it now, could feel it—the deep, ancient wisdom that lay hidden within the earth, the stories that were written in the layers of soil, the roots, the stones, the fossils. It was wisdom that could not be rushed, that could only be uncovered with patience, with careful observation, with a deep respect for the world around him.

As the day wore on and the sun began to dip toward the horizon, Finn and Griselda sat back on the soft, moss-covered ground, their paws dirty and their hearts full. The clearing was quiet and the air still as if the forest itself was listening and waiting for them to understand the lessons it had to offer.

Finn looked over at Griselda, his eyes filled with gratitude. "Thank you," he said softly. "I feel . . . different now. I feel like I'm beginning to understand, like I'm starting to see the world in a new way."

Griselda smiled, her expression warm and knowing. "You are, Finn. You are beginning to see the world as it truly is, not just as it appears on the surface. You are beginning to understand that wisdom is not something that can be

rushed or forced but something that must be nurtured, that must grow slowly, like the roots of a tree deep within the earth."

Finn nodded, the truth of her words resonating deep within him. He knew that he still had much to learn, that the path ahead was long and winding, but he also knew that he was on the right track, that he was beginning to grasp the deeper truths that Griselda was trying to teach him.

As they sat there in the fading light, surrounded by the ancient trees and the rich, fertile earth, Finn felt a deepening sense of peace, of connection. He was no longer just a lone fox on a journey; he was part of something much larger, much older, much wiser. He was a part of Everleaf, a part of the earth, a part of the deep, ancient wisdom that lay hidden within the soil.

And with that understanding came a deep, abiding sense of humility. For Finn knew now that he was just one small part of a much larger, older system—one thread in the vast tapestry of life that made up the forest. And in that knowledge, he found strength, purpose, and wisdom.

The lessons of the earth had begun to take root within him. Finn knew that he would carry them with him on his journey and that they would guide him, nurture him, and help him grow into the fox he was meant to be.

Chapter 4

The First Trial of Patience

T he morning sun filtered gently through the thick canopy of Everleaf, casting dappled shadows on the forest floor. The air was crisp and cool, filled with the scent of pine and earth and the sounds of birds singing a melodic chorus in the distance. Finn walked beside Griselda, the ancient tortoise, who moved with a slow, deliberate grace, her every step a lesson in patience. Finn had learned much from her in the past few days, but today, he sensed, would be different. Today, he would face his first true test.

They had been walking for hours, the forest around them gradually changing from the dense, ancient woods that Finn had come to know, to a more open and barren landscape. The trees grew farther apart here, their branches sparse and

gnarled, the ground beneath them hard and rocky. The path that Finn and Griselda followed was uneven, strewn with stones and tangled roots that jutted out of the earth like the bones of some great, slumbering beast.

Griselda had been silent for most of the journey, her expression calm and unreadable. Finn, too, had remained quiet, his mind occupied with the lessons she had imparted, the wisdom she had shared. But as they continued onward, he couldn't shake the feeling that something was coming—that he was about to face a challenge unlike any he had encountered thus far.

At last, they reached a small clearing where the ground was a mix of hard-packed dirt and jagged rocks. In the center of the clearing stood a large boulder, its surface rough and weathered and covered in patches of moss and lichen. It seemed out of place in the otherwise flat landscape— a solitary monolith that commanded attention.

Griselda came to a stop beside the boulder, her eyes narrowing as she regarded it. Finn followed her gaze, his curiosity piqued. There was something about the boulder, something that drew him in and made him want to explore, to understand its significance.

"This," Griselda said, her voice calm but firm, "is where you will face your first true trial of patience, Finn."

Finn looked at her, his heart quickening with a mix of excitement and apprehension. "What must I do?" he asked, eager to prove himself, to show that he had learned the lessons she had taught him.

The First Trial of Patience

Griselda turned her gaze toward him; her eyes filled with the depth of ages. "You must cross this clearing," she said simply. "But there is a catch. You cannot cross it quickly. If you do, you will fail."

Finn frowned, his mind racing as he tried to make sense of her words. The clearing was not particularly large; it was no more than twenty paces from one side to the other. He could easily cross it in a matter of seconds if he wanted to. But he knew that Griselda's challenges were never as straightforward as they seemed. There was something more to this task, something that required careful thought, observation, and, most importantly, patience.

"Take your time, Finn," Griselda continued, her voice gentle but insistent. "Observe the clearing. Think deeply about what lies ahead. There is more here than meets the eye."

Finn nodded, his mind sharpening with focus. He turned his attention to the clearing, his eyes scanning every detail—the way the ground sloped slightly to the left, the uneven surface of the rocks, and the shadows cast by the boulder in the center. He could feel the weight of the task pressing down on him, the importance of getting it right.

At first, Finn's instinct was to move quickly, to rush across the clearing and reach the other side as quickly as possible. But he stopped himself, remembering Griselda's words. If he acted hastily, he would fail. He needed to slow down, to think carefully, to approach the task with the patience and wisdom that Griselda had been teaching him.

The Tortoise's Timeless Wisdom

He took a deep breath, centering himself, and began to move forward but not toward the center. Instead, he walked slowly around the edge of the clearing, studying the ground as he went. He noticed the small cracks in the earth, the way the stones were arranged in an almost deliberate pattern, as if they had been placed there for a reason.

The boulder in the center drew his attention, its presence commanding yet mysterious. There was something about it, something that felt almost alive, as if it were waiting for him to make a move. But Finn resisted the urge to approach it directly. Instead, he continued his slow, deliberate circuit around the clearing, his mind turning over every possibility, every angle.

As he walked, Finn began to notice something strange. The shadows in the clearing were not quite right. They shifted and changed in a way that didn't match the movement of the sun. The shadows seemed to stretch and twist, creating illusions of depth where there was none, making the clearing appear both larger and smaller than it really was.

He paused, narrowing his eyes as he tried to make sense of what he was seeing. It was as if the clearing itself was playing tricks on him, trying to lure him into a false sense of security. He realized that if he had rushed across the clearing without paying attention, he might have stumbled into one of these illusions, lost his footing, or worse.

Finn's heart pounded in his chest as he continued his careful examination. He crouched down to study the ground more closely, running a paw over the dirt and

stones, feeling for any irregularities. And then he found it—a small indentation in the earth, almost invisible to the naked eye, but unmistakable when touched. It was a pitfall, carefully concealed beneath a thin layer of soil, waiting to trap the unwary.

Finn's breath caught in his throat. He looked around and realized that there were more pitfalls scattered throughout the clearing, each one hidden in plain sight, each one ready to ensnare anyone who moved too quickly, who didn't take the time to observe, to think, to understand.

He stood up slowly, his mind racing with the implications. This was his trial. The clearing was a maze of traps, each one designed to test his patience, his ability to slow down and think carefully before acting. If he had rushed in, if he had tried to cross the clearing without first understanding the dangers, he would have surely failed.

Griselda watched him from her place by the boulder, her expression calm but watchful. She didn't say a word, didn't offer any hints or guidance. This was Finn's trial, and he had to face it on his own.

Taking another deep breath, Finn began to move forward again, this time with even greater caution. He stepped carefully, testing the ground before each movement, his eyes scanning for any sign of danger. It was slow, painstaking work, but Finn knew that it was the only way to succeed. He had to apply the patience and wisdom that Griselda had taught him, had to resist the urge to rush and take the easy way out.

The Tortoise's Timeless Wisdom

As he neared the center of the clearing, Finn could feel the tension in his body, the sweat on his brow. But he didn't let it distract him. He remained focused, calm, and methodical, his mind working through each step and decision with precision.

Finally, after what felt like an eternity, Finn reached the far side of the clearing. He turned back to look at the path he had taken, at the boulder in the center, at the traps he had avoided. He felt a surge of pride and accomplishment. He had done it. He had passed the trial.

Griselda approached him slowly; her eyes filled with approval. "Well done, Finn," she said softly. "You have shown great patience, great wisdom. You took the time to observe, to think, to understand. You have passed your first true trial."

Finn smiled, his heart swelling with a sense of achievement. But more than that, he felt a deep sense of understanding and growth. He had learned that patience was not just about waiting but about seeing, about understanding the world in a way that haste could never allow. He had learned that true wisdom came from slowing down, from taking the time to think deeply and consider all the possibilities before making a move.

As they left the clearing and continued their journey through the forest, Finn felt a renewed sense of purpose and confidence. He knew that there would be more trials ahead, more challenges that would test his patience, his wisdom. But he was ready. He had learned the value of

slowing down, of thinking carefully before acting, and he knew that these lessons would serve him well in the days to come.

The first trial of patience had been difficult, but it had also been a turning point for Finn. He was no longer the impulsive, quick-thinking fox who had started this journey. He was becoming something more—wiser, more thoughtful, more attuned to the world around him. And with each step forward, he knew that he was growing—not just in knowledge but in wisdom, understanding, and the slow, deliberate power of patience.

Chapter 5

The Rhythm of Time

The forest of Everleaf was a living symphony, a harmony of life and death, growth and decay, where every element played its part in the grand design of nature. As Finn walked beside Griselda, he could feel the pulse of the earth beneath his paws. He felt a steady, rhythmic beat that seemed to echo through the trees, the soil, the very air he breathed. It was a rhythm that had been playing since the beginning of time, a cycle that connected all living things to the past, the present, and the future.

Griselda moved with her usual deliberate pace, her eyes scanning the landscape with a gaze that seemed to penetrate the surface of things, seeing not just what was but what had been and what would be. Finn had learned much from her in the days they had spent together, but today, he sensed,

it would be a lesson unlike any other. Today, he would learn about the rhythm of time itself, and how wisdom was found not in constant motion but in understanding the cycles that governed all life.

They came to a small hill that overlooked a vast expanse of forest. The trees stretched out before them like a sea of green, their leaves rustling gently in the breeze. In the distance, Finn could see the Great Willow, its ancient branches swaying with a slow, deliberate grace, as if it were in tune with some cosmic dance that only it could hear.

Griselda stopped at the top of the hill; her gaze fixed on the horizon. "Finn," she began, her voice soft yet filled with the weight of her years, "do you feel it? The rhythm that underlies everything? The pulse of the earth, the cycle of the seasons, the movement of the stars?"

Finn closed his eyes, focusing on the sensations around him. He could feel the gentle rise and fall of the wind, the rustle of leaves, the distant call of a bird. There was a pattern to it, a sense of order that went beyond the random chaos of the world. It was as if everything was moving in time with a beat, a rhythm that connected all living things.

"Yes," Finn replied, his voice barely above a whisper. "I can feel it. It's like the forest is alive, like it's breathing."

Griselda nodded, a small smile playing at the corners of her mouth. "Indeed, it is. The forest, like all of nature, moves in cycles. There is a time for growth and a time for rest, a time for life and a time for death. These cycles are the

foundation of wisdom, for they teach us that nothing lasts forever but that everything has its time and place."

She gestured to the forest below them. "Look at the trees, Finn. See how they grow tall and strong in the spring and summer, their leaves reaching for the sky, their roots digging deep into the earth. But when autumn comes, they begin to shed their leaves, preparing for the long sleep of winter. They do not fight against the coming cold, nor do they rush to grow before their time. They follow the rhythm of the seasons, understanding that rest is as important as growth, that there is a time for everything."

Finn watched the trees, his mind turning over Griselda's words. He had always seen the forest as a place of constant activity, a place where life was always pushing forward, always striving to grow, to expand. But now, he realized that this was only part of the picture. The forest also knew when to slow down, when to wait, and when to conserve its energy for the times it would be needed most.

Griselda continued, her voice, a soothing melody that seemed to blend with the sounds of the forest. "The stars, too, follow their own cycles. They rise and set with the turning of the earth, their light a guide for those who travel by night. But even the stars are not eternal. They are born, they live, and they die, leaving behind the dust that will one day form new stars. This is the rhythm of the universe, the cycle of time that governs all things."

She turned to Finn; her eyes filled with a deep, ancient wisdom. "To truly understand the world, Finn, you must

learn to see these cycles, to feel the rhythm of time as it moves through you. Wisdom is not found in rushing forward, in trying to outpace the turning of the seasons. It is found in understanding when to move and when to wait, when to act and when to rest."

Finn nodded slowly, the truth of her words sinking deep into his heart. He had always been driven by a sense of urgency, a need to keep moving, to keep pushing forward. But now he realized that constant motion had blinded him to the rhythms that governed the world around him. He had been out of sync, rushing when he should have been waiting, acting when he should have been observing.

Griselda began to walk down the hill, and Finn followed, his mind still turning over the lessons she had shared. As they moved through the forest, Finn began to notice the cycles that Griselda had spoken of—the way the trees bent toward the light, the way the leaves fell in time with the changing seasons, the way the animals moved in harmony with the world around them.

They came to a small stream that wound its way through the forest, its waters clear and cool as they bubbled over rocks and fallen branches. Griselda paused at the edge of the stream, her eyes following the flow of the water.

"This stream," she said, her voice thoughtful, "is a perfect example of the rhythm of time. The water flows in cycles, moving from the mountains to the sea, evaporating into the sky, and then falling like rain to begin the journey again. It does not rush, nor does it linger. It moves at its own pace, following the path that time has set for it."

The Rhythm of Time

Finn crouched beside the stream, watching the water as it flowed over the rocks, the ripples creating patterns that seemed almost hypnotic. He could see the rhythm in the movement of the water, the way it danced and swirled, always moving forward but never in haste.

He reached out and dipped a paw into the water, feeling the coolness against his fur. The water flowed around his paw, not in a rush but with a steady, deliberate pace that seemed to carry with it the wisdom of ages.

Griselda watched him, her eyes filled with a quiet satisfaction. "You see, Finn, time is not your enemy. It is your teacher. It shows you when to move and when to wait, when to push forward and when to step back. It is a rhythm that you must learn to feel and understand if you are to grow in wisdom."

Finn nodded, his heart swelling with a newfound understanding. He could feel the rhythm of time in the forest, in the stream, and in the very air he breathed. It was a rhythm that connected all living things, which guided the cycles of life and death, growth and rest.

As they continued their journey through the forest, Finn began to notice the cycles in everything around him—the way the leaves turned golden and fell in the autumn, the way the birds migrated with the changing seasons, the way the stars moved across the night sky. He could see now that the forest thrived not because it was always in motion but because it knew when to move and when to rest, when to grow and when to conserve its energy.

The Tortoise's Timeless Wisdom

The Great Willow's presence seemed to grow stronger as they walked, its ancient branches swaying gently in the breeze, as if in tune with the rhythm of the earth itself. Finn could hear the whispers of the Great Willow, faint but clear, echoing the lessons that Griselda had taught him.

"Wait," the Great Willow seemed to whisper, its voice a soft murmur carried on the wind. "Wait for the right moment. Do not rush; do not force. Let time guide you, let the rhythm of the earth show you the way."

Finn closed his eyes, letting the whispers wash over him, feeling the truth of the words resonate deep within him. He had been so focused on the destination and reaching his goals that he had forgotten to listen to the rhythm of time, to the cycles that governed the world around him.

But now, he understood. He could feel the rhythm of time moving through him, guiding him and teaching him when to act and when to wait, when to push forward and when to step back. It was a rhythm that he would carry with him—a rhythm that would guide him on his journey and lead him to wisdom.

As the sun began to set, casting a golden glow over the forest, Finn and Griselda reached the base of the Great Willow. The ancient tree stood tall and majestic, its roots digging deep into the earth, its branches reaching toward the sky. It was a living embodiment of the cycles of time, a testament to the wisdom that came from understanding the rhythm of life.

The Rhythm of Time

Griselda turned to Finn, her expression serene. "Remember this day, Finn. Remember the lessons of the forest, the rhythm of the earth, the cycles of time. They are your guides, your teachers. Let them lead you, and you will find the wisdom you seek."

Finn nodded, his heart filled with gratitude and a sense of purpose. He knew now that his journey was not just about moving forward but about understanding the rhythms that governed the world around him. He would follow the cycles of time; he would listen to the whispers of the Great Willow; and he would find the wisdom that lay within.

As the first stars appeared in the night sky, Finn sat beneath the Great Willow, feeling the rhythm of time moving through him, connecting him to the earth, the forest, and the universe. He was no longer just a fox on a journey; he was a part of something greater, something timeless, something filled with wisdom.

And with that understanding, Finn knew that he was ready to face whatever lay ahead, with patience, wisdom, and the rhythm of time as his guide.

Chapter 6

The Patience of Stone

The sun had barely begun its ascent, casting long, soft shadows across the forest floor as Finn and Griselda made their way through Everleaf's deepest, most ancient groves. The air was cool and still, with only the occasional rustle of leaves or the distant call of a bird to break the profound silence that enveloped them. There was something different about this part of the forest—an almost sacred stillness that spoke of age, of time that had passed at a pace slower than the mind could fathom.

Griselda moved steadily beside Finn, her gait as measured and deliberate as always, but there was a certain gravity in her movements today. Finn could sense the importance of where they were going, of what he was about to learn. It would be a lesson that required not just his mind but his heart, his soul, and most importantly, his patience.

The Tortoise's Timeless Wisdom

They walked for what felt like hours, the forest growing denser around them; the trees in this part of the forest were taller and older, their trunks thick with the moss and lichens that only centuries could bring. The path beneath their feet became rockier as the soft earth gave way to hard stone that jutted out of the ground like the bones of the earth itself. The air grew cooler and the light dimmer as they descended into a hidden valley that seemed untouched by time.

At last, they reached their destination—a secluded glen surrounded by towering cliffs of stone with surfaces worn smooth by eons of wind and water. The cliffs were a testament to the patience of the earth, to the slow but inexorable power of time. Finn stood at the edge of the glen, his eyes wide with awe as he took in the sight before him.

The stone walls were etched with intricate patterns, grooves, and channels that wound their way across the surface in delicate, flowing lines. It was as if the very rock had been carved by an unseen hand, each mark a record of time's passing. There were places where the stone had been worn away completely, leaving behind hollowed-out caves and archways, their forms graceful and fluid, shaped not by force but by the gentle persistence of nature.

Griselda led Finn to the center of the glen, where a small, crystal-clear stream bubbled up from the ground and wound its way through the rocks, its waters shimmering in the pale light. The stream was quiet, its flow gentle, almost imperceptible, yet Finn could see the effects of its passage all around him. The stones that lined its banks were smooth,

polished to a gleam by the steady, patient movement of water over countless years.

"This place," Griselda said softly, her voice carrying the weight of the ages, "is a place of great power. Not the power of force or speed but the power of patience, of time. These stones, these cliffs, have been shaped over millennia by the gentle, persistent touch of water and wind. They were not carved by sudden impact or violent change but by the slow, steady rhythm of time itself."

Finn knelt beside the stream, a paw tracing the smooth surface of a stone that had been shaped by the water's flow. It was cool to the touch, its surface flawless, as if it had been polished by a master craftsman. Yet, Finn knew that no tool had touched this stone—only time, only patience.

Griselda watched him, her eyes filled with a deep, abiding wisdom. "You see, Finn, even the hardest, most unyielding things in this world can be shaped and transformed. It does not happen quickly, nor does it happen easily. But with patience and persistence, even the strongest stone can be worn down and changed."

Finn looked up at her, his mind slowly absorbing the significance of her words. He had faced many challenges on his journey, many obstacles that had seemed insurmountable. Yet, he had always pushed forward, always tried to find a way through, to conquer whatever stood in his path. But now, he realized that there was another way—a way that required not force but patience, a way

that involved not fighting against the world but moving with it, allowing time to do its work.

Griselda continued, her voice calm and steady. "Life is like these stones, Finn. We are all shaped by the forces around us—by time, by experience, by the world in which we live. Sometimes, those forces are harsh, and they leave their mark on us. But other times, they are gentle, and they mold us slowly, imperceptibly, until we become something new, something stronger, something more beautiful."

She gestured to the cliffs around them; their surfaces etched with the patterns of time. "These stones did not resist the forces that shaped them. They did not fight against the water, the wind. They allowed themselves to be shaped, to be changed. And in that process, they became something greater, something that could only have been created through patience, through time."

Finn nodded, the lesson sinking deep into his heart. He could see now that his journey was not just about overcoming obstacles or pushing through whatever stood in his way. It was also about allowing himself to be shaped by the experiences he encountered, about being patient, about understanding that some things could only be achieved through time.

He stood up, his gaze sweeping across the glen, taking in the smooth stones, the carved cliffs, and the gentle stream. It was a place of profound beauty, a beauty that had been created not by sudden force but by the slow, deliberate work of time. And in that beauty, Finn saw a reflection of his own journey, of the path he was on.

Griselda moved to stand beside him, her presence a comforting weight at his side. "You have learned much, Finn," she said softly, "but there is still more to understand, more to internalize. Patience is not just about waiting; it is about allowing time to work and understanding that not everything can be rushed, that some things must be allowed to unfold in their own time."

Finn turned to her; his eyes filled with determination. "I understand, Griselda," he said, his voice steady. "I know now that I can't rush my journey, that I need to let time shape me, just as it has shaped these stones."

Griselda nodded; her eyes filled with approval. "Good. But remember, Finn, patience is not just about waiting passively. It is also about persistence, about continuing to move forward, even when the progress is slow, even when it seems like nothing is changing. The stream that carved these stones did not stop, did not give up. It kept flowing, kept moving, and in time, it shaped the world around it."

Finn looked at the stream, its waters clear and steady as they flowed over the stones. He could see the truth in Griselda's words—the stream had not forced its way through the stone, but neither had it stopped. It had kept moving, kept flowing, and in doing so, it had created something beautiful, something lasting.

He took a deep breath, allowing the cool air to fill his lungs as the scent of the earth and stone grounded him in the present moment. He knew now that his journey was not just about reaching a destination but about the process, about the way he allowed himself to be shaped by the

experiences he encountered. He needed to be patient, but he also needed to be persistent, to keep moving forward, even when the path was difficult and the progress was slow.

Griselda turned to him, her expression serene. "Remember this, Finn: The patience of stone is not a passive thing. It is a powerful force, one that can shape the hardest, most unyielding elements in the world. But it requires time, and it requires persistence. It is a lesson that you must carry with you on your journey, a lesson that will help you overcome the obstacles that lie ahead."

Finn nodded; his heart filled with a sense of resolve. He knew that there would be times when he would face challenges that seemed insurmountable. But he also knew that with patience and persistence, he could overcome those challenges; he could allow time to shape him and mold him into something stronger, something wiser.

As they left the glen and made their way back through the forest, Finn felt a deep sense of peace settle over him. He was content to let the journey unfold at its own pace, to let time do its work and allow himself to be shaped by the experiences he encountered.

He knew now that the obstacles he faced were not just barriers to be overcome but opportunities for growth, for learning, for transformation. And with that understanding came a sense of purpose and direction. He was not just moving forward; he was becoming something greater, something stronger, something more beautiful.

The Patience of Stone

And as the sun set behind the trees, casting long shadows across the forest floor, Finn felt the rhythm of the earth beneath his paws—the steady, patient pulse of time guiding him on his journey. He was ready to face whatever lay ahead with patience, persistence, and the understanding that even the hardest things in life could be shaped and transformed by the gentle, inexorable power of time.

Chapter 7

The Echoes of the Past

The forest of Everleaf had always been a place of mystery, a living testament to the passage of time and the countless lives that had flourished and faded beneath its towering trees. As Finn and Griselda walked through the ancient woods, there was a weight in the air, a sense of history that pressed down upon them like the dense canopy overhead. Every step they took seemed to stir up echoes of the past, whispering of forgotten stories, of lessons learned through struggle and sacrifice.

Griselda led Finn to a secluded glade where the trees stood like silent sentinels, their bark rough and gnarled, marked by the passage of centuries. The ground beneath their feet was covered in a thick carpet of moss, soft and cool, as if it had grown there undisturbed for countless years. In the center of the glade stood a stone, weathered and worn, its

surface etched with symbols and patterns that Finn couldn't quite decipher. It was a monument to the past, a reminder of the history that had shaped Everleaf and all who lived within it.

Griselda came to a halt beside the stone, her eyes distant as she gazed upon it. Finn could sense the depth of her thoughts as her mind seemed to be reaching back through the layers of time, pulling forth memories that had long been buried beneath the surface.

"Finn," she began, her voice low and resonant, "this place is sacred, not because of what it is but because of what it represents. It is a place where the past speaks to those who are willing to listen, where the mistakes and triumphs of those who came before us echo through the ages, offering their wisdom to those who seek it."

Finn stepped closer to the stone, his eyes tracing the intricate patterns carved into its surface. There was a story here, he realized—a story that had been written long before he was born, a story that held the key to understanding the world around him, and perhaps, his own journey.

Griselda continued; her gaze still fixed on the stone. "Many heroes have walked these woods, Finn. Many have sought wisdom, courage, and strength. But not all of them succeeded. Some were led astray by haste, by ignorance, by the belief that they could bend the world to their will without first understanding it. Their stories are a warning, a reminder that the past is not something to be forgotten but something to be learned from."

She gestured to the stone, her eyes meeting Finn's. "This monument was erected in honor of those who came before us, those who faced great challenges and made great sacrifices. But it is also a reminder of the consequences of their actions—of the mistakes they made, and the lessons they learned too late."

Finn felt a shiver run down his spine as he looked at the stone, the weight of its history closing in on him. He could almost hear the voices of the past, the whispers of those who had walked this path before him as if their words were carried on the wind like the rustling of leaves.

"Tell me about them," Finn said softly, his voice filled with a mix of curiosity and reverence. "Tell me their stories."

Griselda nodded, her expression solemn. "Very well, Finn. I will tell you of the heroes who came before you, and of the lessons they learned—lessons that you must take to heart if you are to succeed in your own journey."

She began to speak, her voice weaving a tapestry of stories that spanned the ages. She spoke of Eolan the Swift, a young fox much like Finn, who had once roamed Everleaf with a heart full of fire and a mind that raced ahead of his paws. Eolan had been driven by a desire to prove himself to be the fastest, the strongest, and the best. He had believed that speed was the key to victory, that if he could outrun his challenges, he would never have to face them.

But Eolan's haste had been his downfall. In his rush to reach his goals, he had failed to see the dangers that lay in his path. He had ignored the warnings of those who had come

before him, believing that he could forge his own way, that he did not need the wisdom of the past. And in the end, his speed had led him straight into a trap—a pitfall hidden by the shadows, where he had fallen and been lost to the darkness.

Griselda's voice was heavy with sorrow as she spoke of Eolan, her eyes reflecting the pain of a lesson learned too late. "Eolan was a hero, yes, but he was also a cautionary tale. He taught us that speed without wisdom is like a blade without a handle—it cuts not only your enemies but yourself. His story is a reminder that haste is not a virtue but a vice, one that blinds you to the dangers that lie ahead."

Finn listened intently, his mind turning over the story of Eolan, seeing the parallels to his own journey. He had always prided himself on his quick thinking, his ability to act swiftly in the face of danger. But now, he saw the danger in that approach, which could lead him into traps of his own making if he wasn't careful.

Griselda continued, her voice taking on a more hopeful tone as she spoke of another hero, Lira the Wise, a deer who had been known for her gentle nature and her deep understanding of the forest. Lira had not been the fastest or the strongest, but she had been patient, and she had listened to the world around her. She had understood that the forest was not just a place to be conquered but a living entity with its own rhythms, its own wisdom.

Lira had faced great challenges in her time, battles that had tested her courage and her resolve. But unlike Eolan, she had not rushed into the fray. She had taken the time to understand her enemies, to learn their weaknesses, and to find the right moment to strike. Her patience had been her greatest weapon, allowing her to outmaneuver those who sought to destroy her, and in the end, she had emerged victorious.

"Lira's story," Griselda said, her voice filled with quiet pride, "teaches us that wisdom is not about knowing everything but about knowing when to act and when to wait. She showed us that true strength lies not in brute force but in understanding the world around you, in seeing the patterns that others miss, and in finding the right moment to move."

Finn felt a deep sense of admiration for Lira, a hero who had succeeded not through speed or strength but through wisdom and patience. He could see the value in her approach, the way it aligned with the lessons Griselda had been teaching him. Lira had understood the rhythms of the forest, the cycles of life and death, and she had used that understanding to her advantage.

As Griselda spoke of other heroes—some who had triumphed, others who had fallen— Finn began to see the importance of the past, the way it shaped the present and the future. Each story was a lesson, a piece of the puzzle that made up the world of Everleaf. The heroes of the past faced challenges much like his own, and their experiences offered invaluable insights into his own journey.

But more than that, Finn began to realize that understanding the past was crucial to shaping the future. The mistakes of

those who had come before him were not just tragedies; they were opportunities to learn, to grow, to avoid the same pitfalls. And the triumphs of the past were not just victories; they were blueprints for success, guides that could help him navigate the challenges that lay ahead.

Griselda finished her stories, her voice trailing off into the silence of the glade. Finn stood quietly beside her, his mind filled with the echoes of the past, the lessons of the heroes who had walked these woods long before him. He felt a deep connection to them, a sense of continuity that stretched across the ages, linking him to the countless souls who had faced the same challenges, the same fears, the same hopes.

"The past," Griselda said softly, her eyes meeting Finn's, "is not just a collection of stories. It is a guide, a teacher, a mirror that shows us who we are and who we can become. The heroes of the past made their choices, for better or for worse, and those choices shaped the world we live in today. But their stories are not finished, Finn. They live on in us, in the choices we make, in the paths we walk."

Finn nodded, his heart heavy with the weight of responsibility but also filled with a sense of purpose. He knew now that his journey was not just about finding his own way but about carrying forward the lessons of the past, about learning from the mistakes and triumphs of those who had come before him. He was part of something greater, something that spanned generations, something that would continue long after he was gone.

The Echoes of the Past

As they left the glade and continued their journey through the forest, Finn felt the presence of the past all around him, echoes of the heroes who had walked through these woods before him. Their stories were a part of him now; their lessons were etched into his soul like the patterns on the stone in the glade. And with that understanding came a renewed sense of determination, a resolve to honor the past by shaping a better future.

The echoes of the past would guide him, would inform him of his choices and help him navigate the challenges that lay ahead. And with each step, Finn knew that he was not alone—that the heroes of Everleaf walked beside him and that their wisdom, courage, mistakes, and triumphs were a part of the tapestry that made up his own journey.

In that moment, Finn understood that the past was not just something to be remembered but something to be lived, to be carried forward into the future. And with that realization, he felt a deep sense of peace, knowing that he was on the right path, that he was part of something timeless, something enduring, something filled with wisdom.

As the sun began to set, casting a golden glow over the forest, Finn and Griselda reached the edge of the Great Willow's domain. The ancient tree stood tall and majestic, its branches swaying gently in the breeze, as if welcoming them back. And as Finn looked up at the Great Willow, he heard its whispers, faint but clear, echoing the lessons he had learned.

The Tortoise's Timeless Wisdom

"Remember the past," the Great Willow seemed to say, its whispers a soft murmur carried on the wind. "For the past is the foundation upon which the future is built. Learn from the heroes who came before you and carry their wisdom with you as you walk your path."

Finn closed his eyes, letting the whispers wash over him, feeling the truth of the words resonate deep within him. He was ready to face whatever lay ahead, with the echoes of the past as his guide, with the wisdom of those who had walked these woods before him as his strength.

And as the first stars appeared in the night sky, Finn knew that he was not just a fox on a journey; he was a part of Everleaf's history, a part of its future, a part of the timeless cycle that connected all who lived within its ancient, whispering woods.

Chapter 8

The Weight of Time

The days in Everleaf had grown longer, or so it seemed to Finn. The once vibrant forest, filled with the thrill of discovery and the promise of adventure, now felt like a labyrinth of endless lessons, each one demanding more of him than the last. The slow, deliberate pace that Griselda had taught him—the patience that he had begun to cultivate—was starting to feel like a burden, a weight pressing down on his spirit with every step.

The sun hung low in the sky as Finn and Griselda made their way through a part of the forest that was darker, denser, and quieter than any they had traversed. The trees here were ancient, their gnarled roots twisting and turning through the earth like the fingers of some giant, unseen hand. The air was thick with the scent of moss and decay,

and the only sound was the soft rustling of leaves overhead, as if the forest itself was holding its breath, waiting.

Finn's paws dragged along the ground, his energy sapped not by physical exertion but by the constant mental and emotional effort required to absorb the lessons that Griselda imparted. He could feel the weight of knowledge pressing down on him—the slow, relentless march of time that seemed to stretch out endlessly before him. The excitement of his journey had faded, replaced by a deep weariness that gnawed at his resolve.

Griselda, as always, moved with her steady, deliberate pace, her expression calm and focused. But even she seemed to sense Finn's growing fatigue, his frustration with the slow progress they were making. She paused at the base of a large, weathered tree, turning to look at him with eyes that seemed to pierce through his outer shell, seeing the turmoil within.

"Finn," she said gently, her voice a balm to his weary soul, "I can see that you are tired, that the weight of this journey is beginning to bear down on you. It is natural to feel this way, to question whether you have the strength to continue. But understand this: It is in carrying this weight that you will find your true strength."

Finn looked at her, his eyes filled with doubt. "But it's so heavy, Griselda," he replied, his voice strained. "The lessons, the patience, the constant waiting . . . it feels like I'm walking in circles, like I'm not getting anywhere. I don't know if I can keep going like this."

The Weight of Time

Griselda nodded slowly, her gaze thoughtful. "I know it feels that way, Finn. The burden of knowledge, of time, can be heavy. It can make you feel as if you are moving through molasses, each step harder than the last. But this weight, this burden, is also a gift. It is through carrying it that you build the strength to face the challenges ahead."

She gestured to the ground around them, where the roots of the trees wove together in a complex, tangled web. "Look at these roots, Finn. They are thick, twisted, and heavy, but they are also the foundation of these great trees. Without them, the trees would fall, unable to stand against the storms that come their way. The weight they carry is what gives them their strength, their stability."

Finn gazed at the roots, seeing in them a reflection of his own journey. He could feel the truth in Griselda's words, but the weariness in his heart made it difficult to fully embrace the lesson. The weight he carried felt like it was crushing him, dragging him down into the earth, rather than lifting him up.

Sensing his struggle, Griselda moved closer, her eyes soft with understanding. "There is something I want to show you, Finn," she said, her voice low and calm. "Something that may help you understand the true nature of the burden you carry."

She led him deeper into the forest, to a place where the trees grew even taller, and the shadows stretched long and dark across the forest floor. In the center of a small clearing stood a large stone, smooth and round, its surface polished

to a gleam by time and the elements. It was a beautiful, ancient artifact, yet it exuded a sense of gravity, of weight that went beyond the physical.

"This stone," Griselda explained, "has been here for longer than even I can remember. It was once part of a great mountain, a piece of the earth that was unyielding, immovable. But over time, the wind, the rain, and the flow of water shaped it, smoothed its edges, and turned it into what you see before you."

She paused, allowing Finn to take in the sight, to feel the significance of the stone. "I want you to carry this stone, Finn. Not far, just to the edge of the clearing. I want you to feel its weight, to understand what it means to carry something that has been shaped by time."

Finn hesitated, his heart sinking at the thought of adding another burden to his already weary body. But he trusted Griselda, and he knew that this was an important part of his journey, another lesson that he needed to learn.

He approached the stone, placing his paws on its smooth surface. It was cool to the touch, solid and unyielding, yet there was a sense of life in it, as if it carried within it the memory of the mountain from which it had come. With a deep breath, Finn wrapped his arms around the stone and began to lift.

The stone was heavy—heavier than anything Finn had ever lifted before. It pressed down on him with an almost unbearable force, his muscles straining as he struggled to rise to his feet. But he could also feel the stone's history, the

countless years it had endured, the patience with which it had been shaped by the elements. It was a burden, yes, but it was also a testament to the power of time, to the strength that could be found in carrying such a weight.

Step by step, Finn began to move, his body trembling with the effort. The weight of the stone pressed down on him, but with each step, he could feel something changing within him. The stone was not just a burden; it was a challenge, a test of his resolve, his patience, his willingness to endure.

Griselda watched him, her expression calm but watchful. She knew that this was a moment of transformation for Finn, a moment when he would begin to understand the true nature of the journey he was on.

As Finn reached the edge of the clearing, his legs nearly buckling under the weight, he paused, his breath coming in ragged gasps. The stone seemed to grow heavier with each passing moment, the burden of time and knowledge pressing down on him like a physical force. But he did not let go. He held on, feeling the weight, the history, the power of the stone.

And then, in a moment of clarity, Finn understood. The weight he carried was not just physical; it was the weight of time, of the lessons he had learned, the experiences he had gained. It was a burden, yes, but it was also a source of strength, a foundation upon which he could build his future. The stone was heavy, but it was also solid, enduring, unbreakable. And in carrying it, Finn realized that he was not just learning patience; he was

becoming strong, resilient, capable of withstanding whatever challenges lay ahead.

With a final, exhausted push, Finn lowered the stone to the ground, his body trembling with the effort. He stood there, panting, sweat dripping from his brow, but there was a sense of triumph in his heart, a deep understanding that had taken root within him.

Griselda approached; her eyes filled with pride. "You have done well, Finn," she said softly. "You have carried the weight of time, and in doing so, you have begun to understand its true nature. The burden you carry is not just a weight; it is a source of strength, of wisdom. It is through carrying this weight that you will find the power to continue your journey, to face the challenges that lie ahead."

Finn looked up at her, his eyes shining with a new resolve. "I understand now, Griselda," he said, his voice steady despite his exhaustion. "The weight of time, the burden of knowledge . . . it's not something to be feared. It's something to be embraced, to be carried with pride. Because it's through carrying this weight that I will become stronger, wiser, more capable of fulfilling my purpose."

Griselda nodded; her expression was serene. "Yes, Finn. Time can feel heavy, and the journey can be long and difficult. But it is through carrying that weight that you will grow and build the strength you need to succeed. Do not fear the burden; embrace it, and let it shape you, as the stone has been shaped by the elements."

The Weight of Time

Finn felt a deep sense of peace settle over him, the weariness in his heart replaced by a quiet determination. He knew that the journey ahead would not be easy—that there would be times when the weight of his responsibilities would feel almost unbearable. But he also knew that he had the strength to carry that weight; endure the slow, deliberate pace of his journey; and find the wisdom that lay at the end.

As they left the clearing and continued their journey through the forest, Finn could still feel the weight of the stone in his arms, a reminder of the lesson he had learned. But now, that weight was not a burden; it was a symbol of his strength, his resilience, his ability to carry the lessons of the past and use them to shape his future.

And with each step, Finn felt the rhythm of time moving through him, guiding him, teaching him, making him stronger. He was no longer just a fox on a journey. He was a bearer of wisdom; a carrier of the weight of time; a symbol of the strength that could be found in patience, endurance, and the slow, deliberate power of growth.

As the sun set behind the trees, casting a golden glow over the forest, Finn knew that he was ready to face whatever lay ahead with the weight of time as his guide and the strength of his journey as his foundation.

Chapter 9

The Council of Elders

The sun had barely begun to rise, casting long shadows across the forest floor, as Finn made his way to the heart of Everleaf. The path ahead of him was lined with ancient trees, their branches intertwining above to form a canopy so thick that it allowed only the faintest rays of sunlight to penetrate. The air was cool and still, filled with the soft rustling of leaves and the distant calls of the forest's creatures waking to the new day.

Finn's heartbeat steadily in his chest, but there was an undercurrent of anxiety threading through his thoughts. Today was not just another day in his journey. Today, he would stand before the Council of Elders, the wisest and most revered creatures of Everleaf to have his progress evaluated. These were the beings who had watched over

the forest for countless generations, whose knowledge and experience spanned centuries. To stand before them was both an honor and a daunting responsibility.

As Finn approached the clearing where the Council would gather, he could feel the weight of the moment. The lessons he had learned from Griselda, the patience he had cultivated, the understanding he had gained—all of it would be tested today. That thought was both exhilarating and terrifying. He had come so far, yet he knew there was still much to learn, much to prove.

The clearing itself was a place of serene beauty, a natural amphitheater formed by the towering trees that ringed it. In the center stood a massive stone table, worn smooth by the passage of time, its surface etched with the symbols of the forest's ancient lore. Around it, seats fashioned from the roots of trees rose from the ground, each one marked with the insignia of the elder who would sit there. The entire scene exuded an air of gravitas, as if the very earth recognized the significance of what was to take place.

Finn hesitated at the edge of the clearing, his breath catching in his throat as he caught sight of the elders beginning to arrive. They moved with a grace and dignity that spoke of their years, their presence commanding respect without a single word. There was Haldor, the great owl, whose eyes had seen more than any other creature in the forest; Seraphina, the ancient deer, whose wisdom was known far and wide; and of course, Griselda, whose teachings had guided Finn to this very moment.

One by one, the elders took their places around the stone table, their movements slow and deliberate, as if time itself had slowed to honor their gathering. Finn watched them, feeling both small and significant at the same time. He was a part of something much larger than himself, a thread in the vast tapestry of Everleaf's history, and yet, today, he would be the focus of their attention.

Griselda caught Finn's eye as she settled into her seat, giving him a small, encouraging nod. It was a gesture of reassurance, a reminder that he was not alone in this and that the lessons he had learned would guide him through whatever was to come. Finn took a deep breath, steadying himself before stepping into the clearing.

The elders' eyes turned to him as he approached the stone table, their gazes filled with a mixture of curiosity, respect, and quiet expectation. Finn could feel the weight of their scrutiny, but he did not shy away. He stood tall, his head held high, ready to face whatever they had to say.

Haldor, the owl, was the first to speak, his voice deep and resonant, carrying with it the authority of countless years. "Finn, you stand before us today as one who has embarked on a journey of great significance. You have walked the paths of Everleaf, learned the lessons of patience and time, and faced trials that would have broken many. We gather here to hear of your progress, to share our insights, and to guide you on the path that lies ahead."

Finn bowed his head respectfully, acknowledging the elder's words. "I am honored to stand before you, Haldor,

and before all of you, wise elders of Everleaf. I have learned much, but I know that my journey is far from complete. I seek your wisdom and your guidance, so that I may continue to grow and fulfill the role that I have been given."

Seraphina, the deer, spoke next, her voice gentle but firm, like the rustling of leaves in a summer breeze. "We have watched you, Finn, from the moment you took your first steps on this path. We have seen your struggles, your doubts, your moments of weakness, but we have also seen your growth, your courage, and your strength. The lessons you have learned from Griselda are not easy ones, but they are the foundation upon which true wisdom is built."

Finn nodded, his heart swelling with a mixture of pride and humility. He had indeed struggled; there had been moments when he had doubted himself, when the weight of the journey had seemed too much to bear. But each time, he had found the strength to continue, to learn from his mistakes, to push forward despite the challenges.

Griselda's voice, calm and steady, cut through the quiet of the clearing. "Finn has shown great promise, but there is still much for him to learn. The path he walks is not an easy one, and it will require all the strength, patience, and wisdom that he can muster. But I believe that he is capable, that he has within him the qualities of a leader, the potential to guide others as he has been guided."

The other elders nodded in agreement, their expressions thoughtful. Finn could feel their eyes on him, weighing his worth, his potential. It was a moment of intense

vulnerability but also one of immense opportunity. He was being seen, truly seen, for the first time—not just as a young fox on a journey, but as a potential leader, a figure who could one day stand among them as an equal.

Haldor leaned forward, his sharp eyes fixed on Finn. "Leadership is not just about strength, Finn. It is about understanding the needs of those you lead, about making decisions that benefit the whole, not just the individual. It is about patience, about knowing when to act and when to wait. These are lessons you have begun to learn, but they are lessons that must be practiced, honed, until they become a part of who you are."

Finn met the owl's gaze, feeling the truth of his words resonate deep within him. Leadership was not just about being strong or brave; it was about wisdom and the ability to see the bigger picture, understand the needs of the community, and act in ways that would benefit all. It was a heavy responsibility, one that Finn was beginning to feel he could bear.

Seraphina spoke again; her voice filled with warmth. "You have already begun to lead, Finn, even if you do not yet realize it. Your actions and choices have a ripple effect throughout Everleaf. The way you carry yourself, the way you face your challenges—these are all lessons that others will learn from and follow. Do not underestimate the impact you have, even now, as you continue to grow and learn."

Finn felt a surge of emotion at her words and a deep sense of responsibility mingled with growing confidence. He had

not seen himself as a leader before, but now, standing before the elders, he could see the path beginning to take shape. It was not a path he had chosen but one that had chosen him—a path that required not just strength but wisdom, patience, and an understanding of the world around him.

Griselda looked at Finn with a quiet intensity. "You have learned much, Finn, but there is one more lesson that you must take to heart. Leadership is not just about guiding others; it is about carrying their burdens as well. The weight of leadership can be heavy, but it is through carrying that weight that you will find your true strength. You must be willing to bear the responsibility of others and make decisions that will affect not just yourself but the entire community."

Finn nodded, his resolve hardening. He could feel the weight of Griselda's words, the truth in them. Leadership was not just about being at the forefront; it was about supporting those who followed, about being a pillar of strength that others could rely on. It was a burden, yes, but it was also a privilege, a role that he was beginning to understand he could fulfill.

The elders sat in silence for a moment, their eyes on Finn, as if they were collectively assessing his readiness for the path that lay ahead. Finn stood tall, his heart steady, his mind clear. He was ready to accept whatever they decided, to continue his journey with the lessons they had imparted.

Finally, Haldor spoke, his voice a deep, resonant echo that seemed to vibrate through the very ground beneath them.

"Finn, we acknowledge the growth you have shown and the wisdom you have begun to cultivate. You are on the right path, but there is still much for you to learn. We will continue to watch over you and guide you, but know that the choices you make from here on out will define not just your own journey but the future of Everleaf."

Finn bowed deeply, his heart filled with gratitude and a renewed sense of purpose. "Thank you, wise elders. I will do my best to honor the lessons you have taught me and to lead with wisdom, patience, and strength. I will carry the weight of this responsibility with pride, and I will strive to be worthy of the trust you have placed in me."

Seraphina smiled, her eyes filled with warmth and kindness. "We believe in you, Finn. You have the heart of a leader, the spirit of one who can guide others through the challenges that lie ahead. Trust in yourself, and trust in the wisdom you have gained. The path is long, but you are not alone; you have us, and you have the strength within you to succeed."

Griselda nodded, her gaze softening as she looked at Finn. "Remember, Finn, that leadership is not about perfection; it is about growth, about learning from your mistakes and continuing to move forward. You have already shown that you are capable of this, and I have no doubt that you will continue to grow into the leader that Everleaf needs."

Finn felt a deep sense of peace settle over him, the weight of the journey ahead balanced by the strength he had gained from the lessons of the past. He was ready to continue, to face whatever challenges lay ahead, knowing that he was

not alone and that he had the support of the elders and the wisdom they imparted.

As the Council of Elders concluded their gathering, the sun began to rise higher in the sky, casting a warm, golden light over the clearing. Finn stood at the center, feeling the warmth on his fur, the strength of the earth beneath his paws, and the knowledge that he was on the right path.

He was no longer just a fox on a journey—he was a leader in the making who would guide others through the challenges of life with the wisdom of the past and the strength of his convictions as his foundation.

And as the elders began to disperse, their expressions filled with quiet approval, Finn knew that he was ready for whatever lay ahead, with the lessons of the past as his guide and the support of the community as his strength. Finn would walk the path with the wisdom of Everleaf in his heart and the promise of a brighter future on the horizon.

Chapter 10

The Test of Timeless Wisdom

The forest of Everleaf stood in silent anticipation as Finn made his way through its ancient paths. The leaves whispered secrets that only the wind could understand; the roots of the trees were tangled beneath the earth like the thoughts swirling in Finn's mind. He had faced many trials on his journey and learned lessons that had deepened his understanding of time, patience, and wisdom. But today, as he walked with a quiet determination, Finn knew that his greatest challenge still lay ahead.

Griselda, who had been his constant guide, walked beside him in silence. There was a weight in the air, a sense of finality that made Finn's heart beat a little faster. The sun hung low in the sky, casting long shadows that seemed to stretch endlessly into the distance. Everything about this

day felt different—heavier, more profound—as if the very fabric of the forest was holding its breath, waiting for what was to come.

They reached a clearing that Finn had never seen before, a place where the trees parted to reveal a wide expanse of soft grass, dotted with wildflowers. In the center of the clearing stood a single, massive stone, its surface smooth and worn by the passage of time. It was a stone that seemed to carry the weight of ages, as if it had stood there for millennia, watching the world change around it, yet remaining steadfast and unyielding.

Griselda stopped at the edge of the clearing, her expression calm and inscrutable. Finn looked at her, waiting for the guidance that had always come so naturally from her, but she remained silent, her eyes focused on the stone in the center of the clearing.

"This is where your test begins, Finn," Griselda said at last, her voice soft but firm. "But this time, I cannot guide you. You must face this challenge alone, with nothing but the wisdom you have gained to see you through."

Finn felt a shiver run down his spine, not of fear but of the enormity of what lay before him. He had come so far, learned so much, but now it was time to put those lessons to the ultimate test. He looked at the stone, its presence both intimidating and reassuring, a symbol of the endurance and patience he had been cultivating.

"What must I do?" Finn asked, his voice steady but filled with an undercurrent of anxiety.

The Test of Timeless Wisdom

Griselda shook her head slowly. "This test is not about doing, Finn. It is about being. You must remain still, allow the world around you to move, to unfold as it will. You must resist the urge to act, to interfere. You must trust in the wisdom of time, in the power of patience, and allow events to take their course."

Finn nodded, his heart pounding in his chest. He had always been a creature of action, quick to move, to respond, to solve problems as they arose. But now, he was being asked to do the one thing that went against his very nature—to wait, to remain still, to trust that things would unfold as they should, without his intervention.

Griselda stepped back; her eyes filled with a quiet confidence. "You have learned much, Finn. You have the strength within you to succeed. But this is a test that only you can pass, a test that requires you to draw upon everything you have learned about time, patience, and wisdom. I will be here, watching, but I cannot help you. This is your journey."

Finn took a deep breath, steeling himself for the trial ahead. He walked slowly toward the stone in the center of the clearing, each step feeling heavier than the last. When he reached the stone, he placed his paw on its cool, smooth surface, feeling the solid, unyielding strength beneath his touch. The stone held a strength that had been forged over countless years, shaped by the elements, by time itself.

He sat down beside the stone, his back resting against its reassuring presence, and closed his eyes. The world around

him was quiet, the sounds of the forest muted as if the trees and creatures were respecting the gravity of the moment. Finn felt the earth beneath him, the solid ground that had supported him throughout his journey, the same ground that had supported countless others before him.

Time seemed to stretch out, each moment lingering longer than the last. Finn could feel the passage of time in a way he never had before: Time was not as something to be rushed through but something to be experienced fully, deeply with an awareness that transcended the immediate. He listened to the sounds of the forest, the rustling of leaves, the distant calls of birds, the soft whisper of the wind as it moved through the trees. All of it was part of the same rhythm, the same cycle that had been playing out for eons.

As the minutes turned into hours, Finn felt the urge to move, to do something, anything, to break the stillness that surrounded him. His muscles twitched, and his mind raced, searching for a reason to act. But he knew that to give in to that impulse would be to fail the test. This was not a trial of action but of endurance, of trust in the process, in the wisdom of time.

The sun moved slowly across the sky, casting shifting shadows across the clearing. Finn remained still, his breath steady, his mind focused on the lessons he had learned. He remembered the stories of the past, the mistakes of those who had acted in haste, who had tried to force outcomes instead of allowing them to unfold naturally. He thought of Eolan, who had rushed headlong into danger, and of Lira, who had waited, listened, and understood the importance of timing.

The Test of Timeless Wisdom

Hours passed, and the sun began to set, painting the sky with hues of orange and red. Finn felt the cool evening air settle over him, the light fading as the shadows grew longer. His body ached from the stillness; his mind was weary from the effort of holding back the urge to act. But he held on, drawing strength from the lessons of patience and wisdom that Griselda had taught him.

As the last light of day slipped below the horizon, Finn felt a change in the air, a subtle shift in the energy around him. The forest seemed to hold its breath, the stillness deepening, as if waiting for something to happen. Finn opened his eyes, his senses heightened, attuned to the slightest movement, the smallest sound.

And then, in the darkness, he saw it—a flicker of light, faint at first, but growing stronger. It was a firefly, its tiny body glowing softly as it hovered in the air before him. Finn watched as more fireflies appeared, their lights dancing in the night, creating a mesmerizing pattern of movement and light.

The fireflies circled around him, their glow illuminating the clearing, casting the stone in a soft, ethereal light. Finn felt a sense of wonder, of awe, as he watched them move, their delicate wings beating in perfect harmony with the rhythm of the night. It was a dance of time, patience, and wisdom, a testament to the beauty that could only be revealed through stillness, through allowing the world to unfold as it would.

The Tortoise's Timeless Wisdom

In that moment, Finn understood. The test was not about resisting the urge to act but about trusting in the process, in the natural unfolding of events. It was about understanding that sometimes, the greatest wisdom lay not in what you did but in what you didn't do. It was about recognizing that time had its own wisdom, its own rhythm, and that by aligning yourself with it, you could find the answers you sought.

The fireflies continued their dance, their light a reminder of the lessons Finn had learned. He had passed the test— not by doing but by being, by trusting in the wisdom of time, by allowing events to unfold naturally, without interference. He had learned that true strength was not found in action alone but in patience, in the ability to wait, to endure, to trust.

As the night deepened, the fireflies slowly began to disperse, their lights fading into the darkness. Finn watched them go, a deep sense of peace settling over him. He had faced his greatest trial, and he had succeeded. Not by force, not by action but by trusting in the timeless wisdom that Griselda had taught him.

Griselda stepped forward; her eyes filled with pride. "You have done well, Finn," she said softly, her voice carrying the warmth of a thousand suns. "You have learned the most important lesson of all—that sometimes, the greatest wisdom is found in stillness, in allowing the world to move around you, in trusting that time will bring the answers you seek."

The Test of Timeless Wisdom

Finn looked at her, his heart filled with gratitude, with a deep understanding of the journey he had undertaken. "Thank you, Griselda," he replied, his voice steady and sure. "I understand now. I understand that true wisdom is not just about knowing what to do but knowing when to do nothing. It's about trusting in the process, in the rhythm of time, and allowing events to unfold as they will."

Griselda nodded, her eyes shining with approval. "You have learned well, Finn. You are ready for the next step in your journey, whatever it may be. Remember this lesson and carry it with you always. It will serve you well, in ways you cannot yet imagine."

Finn stood beside the stone, the cool night air wrapping around him like a comforting embrace. He had faced his greatest test, and he had emerged stronger, wiser, more in tune with the world around him. The weight of time no longer felt like a burden but like a gift, a source of strength that would guide him through whatever lay ahead.

As the first light of dawn began to break on the horizon, Finn knew that he was ready to face the challenges of the future, ready to lead with wisdom and patience, ready to trust in the timeless rhythm that had guided him thus far. And with that knowledge, he took a deep breath, allowing the air to fill his lungs with the promise of a new day, a new chapter in his journey.

The test of timeless wisdom had been passed, and Finn was ready for whatever lay ahead, with the lessons of the past as his guide and the strength of his own heart as his compass.

Chapter 11

Griselda's Legacy

The dawn light filtered through the dense canopy of Everleaf, casting a soft, golden glow on the forest floor. Finn walked beside Griselda, the ancient tortoise who had been his mentor, his guide, and his steady anchor in the storm of his journey. The lessons he had learned and the wisdom he had gained felt like stones carefully placed in the foundation of his soul, giving him a new sense of purpose, a deeper understanding of his role in the world.

But today, as they moved through the familiar paths of the forest, there was a sense of something new, something shifting. Finn could feel it in the air, a quiet anticipation, as if the trees themselves were waiting for the next chapter of his journey to unfold. And as they walked, Griselda's usual

silence felt heavier, more contemplative as if she too was preparing for something momentous.

They arrived at a secluded glade, a place that Finn had come to associate with moments of profound learning and transformation. The glade was quiet and serene with only the soft rustle of leaves and the distant call of birds to break the stillness. It was a place of reflection and connection to the ancient rhythms of the earth, where time seemed to slow down, allowing every moment to stretch out and be fully experienced.

Griselda stopped at the center of the glade, her wise eyes scanning the surroundings before turning to Finn. There was something different in her gaze today—a depth of emotion that Finn hadn't seen before, a tenderness that spoke of endings and new beginnings.

"Finn," Griselda began, her voice carrying the weight of years, of experiences that spanned lifetimes, "you have come far on your journey. You have faced trials that tested your patience, your strength, your wisdom. You have learned to move with the rhythm of time, understanding the importance of stillness and allowing the world to unfold as it will. But there is one more lesson that you must learn before your journey can continue."

Finn looked at her, his heart beating with a quiet intensity. He knew that whatever she was about to say would mark a turning point, not just in his journey but in his understanding of himself and his place in the world.

Griselda's eyes softened as she spoke. "Wisdom is not just something you gain, Finn. It is something you pass on. The knowledge you have acquired, the lessons you have learned—they are not yours to keep but yours to share. That is the true purpose of wisdom: to guide, to teach, to help others find their own path, just as you have found yours."

Finn's heart swelled with the truth of her words. He had always seen his journey as a personal quest, a path he walked alone. But now, standing in the quiet of the glade, he realized that his journey was part of something much larger, something that connected him to every creature in Everleaf, to the wisdom of the past and the promise of the future.

Griselda continued, her voice growing softer, more reflective. "I was not always the wise old tortoise you see before you. I too was once young, eager, filled with questions and doubts. I sought knowledge just as you do now, and I was guided by those who came before me, who shared their wisdom and helped me find my way. And now, it is my time to pass that wisdom on to you, to help you carry it forward, to ensure that it does not end with me but continues to grow and flourish in the hearts and minds of those who will come after us."

Finn felt a lump rise in his throat as he listened to Griselda's words. He had always seen her as a figure of unshakable strength and endless wisdom, someone who had always been and always would be. But now, he saw her as something more. Griselda was someone who had walked the path before him, learned, struggled, and been shaped by time and experience just as he was being shaped now.

The Tortoise's Timeless Wisdom

Griselda reached into a small pouch she carried at her side, pulling out a simple, yet beautifully crafted pendant. It was made of smooth, polished stone with intricate carvings that seemed to tell a story of their own. She held it out to Finn, her eyes filled with a mix of pride and sadness.

"This," she said, her voice trembling slightly, "was given to me by my mentor, many years ago. It is a symbol of the wisdom that has been passed down through generations, from one guide to the next. And now, it is time for me to pass it on to you, Finn. It is not just a token; it is a mantle, a responsibility. By accepting it, you are accepting the role of a guide, a teacher, someone who will one day pass on the wisdom you have gained to others who seek their way."

Finn's paws trembled as he reached out to take the pendant, the weight of its significance pressing down on him. He could feel the history in it, the countless lives it had touched, the wisdom it had carried through the ages. As he held it in his paws, he felt a deep connection to Griselda, to her mentor, and to all those who had come before them, each one a link in the unbroken chain of wisdom that stretched back through time.

Tears welled in Finn's eyes as he looked at Griselda, the realization of what she was entrusting to him sinking in. "I don't know if I'm ready," he whispered, his voice choked with emotion. "I've learned so much, but I still have so much to learn. How can I guide others when I'm still finding my own way?"

Griselda smiled, her eyes shining with compassion. "None of us are ever truly ready, Finn. We are all always learning,

always growing. But that is the beauty of wisdom—it is not about having all the answers but about seeking them, about walking the path with an open heart and a willingness to learn. You have that within you, Finn. You have the strength, the patience, the wisdom to guide others, just as I have guided you."

Finn nodded, tears slipping down his cheeks as he clutched the pendant to his chest. He felt a profound sense of responsibility but also a deep sense of honor. Griselda was not just passing on a piece of jewelry; she was passing on her legacy, her trust, her belief in him. And Finn knew that he would carry that legacy with pride, that he would do everything in his power to honor the wisdom she had shared with him.

Griselda stepped closer, placing a gentle paw on Finn's shoulder. "You will make mistakes, Finn. We all do. But it is in those mistakes that we find the greatest lessons, the deepest wisdom. And you will not be alone. You have the wisdom of Everleaf within you, the guidance of those who have walked this path before you. Trust in that, and trust in yourself."

Finn took a deep breath, feeling the weight of the pendant in his paws, the weight of the responsibility he was taking on. But he also felt a sense of peace, a sense of purpose. He knew that his journey was far from over, that there were still many lessons to learn, many challenges to face. But he also knew that he was not alone, that he was part of something much larger, something timeless and enduring.

The Tortoise's Timeless Wisdom

Griselda smiled, and her eyes filled with a quiet pride. "You have learned well, Finn. You are ready for the next chapter of your journey, whatever it may be. And one day, when the time is right, you will pass on what you have learned to those who come after you. That is the true legacy of wisdom; it is not something that ends with us but something that lives on, that grows and flourishes in the hearts and minds of others."

Finn nodded, his heart swelling with a sense of determination, of resolve. Although he had a long way to go and many challenges ahead, he knew that he had the strength, the patience, and the wisdom to face them. And he knew that he would carry Griselda's legacy with him, that he would honor the trust she had placed in him, that he would pass on the wisdom he had gained to others, just as she had done for him.

As the sun began to set, Finn stood beside Griselda, the pendant clutched tightly in his paws. He felt a deep sense of connection to her, to the forest, to the countless lives that had been touched by the wisdom of Everleaf. Griselda's legacy was now his to carry, his to pass on. And as the first stars appeared in the night sky, Finn knew that he would do so with pride, with honor, and with the strength that came from knowing he was part of something timeless, something that would endure long after he was gone.

The Dawn of Understanding

The first light of dawn began to break over Everleaf, casting a gentle glow across the forest that Finn had come to know so intimately. The trees, with their ancient branches reaching skyward, seemed to stretch out in a silent greeting to the new day. The air was crisp and still, carrying with it the scent of dew and earth, a reminder of the cycles of time that had governed the forest for millennia.

Finn stood at the edge of a small hill, overlooking the vast expanse of Everleaf. From this vantage point, he could see the Great Willow in the distance, its massive branches swaying softly in the morning breeze. It was a sight that had always filled him with a sense of awe, but today, it carried with it a deeper meaning, a resonance that echoed through his soul.

The Tortoise's Timeless Wisdom

He had walked a long path to reach this moment. The trials he had faced, the lessons he had learned, and the wisdom he had gained—all of it had shaped him, molding him into something more than he had been before. But as he stood there, with the dawn breaking over the horizon, Finn realized that this was not the end of his journey. It was, in fact, just the beginning.

The journey of wisdom, he understood now, was not a destination but a path—one that would continue to unfold before him, revealing new challenges, new lessons, and new opportunities for growth. The patience he had cultivated and the understanding he had gained were tools that would serve him well in the days to come, but they were not the culmination of his journey. They were the foundation upon which he would build the next stages of his life.

As he reflected on this, Finn felt a sense of peace settled over him. The anxiety and doubt that had once plagued him had been replaced by quiet confidence, a certainty that whatever lay ahead, he would face it with the strength and wisdom he had gained. He knew that there would be moments of difficulty and uncertainty, but he also knew that he had the tools to navigate them, the patience to wait for the right moment and the wisdom to see the broader picture.

The Great Willow, standing tall in the distance, seemed to whisper to him in the wind. Finn closed his eyes, letting the soft murmur of its ancient voice wash over him. The whispers were faint, almost indistinct, but they carried with them a sense of reassurance, a reminder that the journey

was far from over, that there was still much to learn, much to discover.

"Finn," the whispers seemed to say, "your journey has only just begun. The wisdom you have gained is but the first step on a path that will stretch out before you for as long as you walk it. Do not rush; do not force. Let the world unfold as it will, and you will find the answers you seek. Trust in the rhythm of time, in the cycles of life, and you will continue to grow, to learn, to become."

Finn opened his eyes, the light of dawn brightening the world around him. He could feel the truth in the Great Willow's words, the quiet certainty that had taken root in his heart. His journey was not about reaching an end point but about continuing to walk the path, about allowing himself to be shaped by the experiences he encountered, and about passing on the wisdom he gained to others who would one day walk the same path.

As he thought of Griselda and the legacy, she had passed on to him, he felt a deep sense of gratitude. She had been his guide and his mentor, but more than that, she had been a bridge between the past and the future, a link in the unbroken chain of wisdom that connected him to the countless creatures who had walked this path before him. And now, it was his turn to carry that legacy forward, to become a guide for others, just as she had been for him.

The thought filled him with a sense of purpose and responsibility but also with a sense of peace. He knew that he would not walk this path alone, that the wisdom

of Everleaf, the guidance of the Great Willow, and the strength of those who had come before him would be with him every step of the way.

As the sun rose higher in the sky, casting its golden light across the forest, Finn felt a surge of hope and anticipation. He looked out over the horizon, his heart swelling with the knowledge that the future was wide open, filled with possibilities that he could not yet see but that he would face with courage and wisdom.

The world was vast, and there were many paths to walk, many lessons to learn, many challenges to overcome. But Finn knew that he was ready to continue his journey, ready to face whatever came next, with the strength of his heart and the wisdom of Everleaf as his guide.

He took a deep breath, filling his lungs with the crisp morning air, and felt the rhythm of the forest, the pulse of life that connected him to everything around him. It was a rhythm that he had come to understand, to trust, to move with rather than against. It was a rhythm that would guide him through the days to come, through the challenges that lay ahead, and through moments of doubt and triumph.

Finn turned his gaze back to the Great Willow, its ancient branches swaying gently in the breeze. The whispers had faded, but their message remained clear in his heart. The journey was not over; it was only just beginning. And with that knowledge, Finn felt a deep sense of peace, of readiness, of quiet confidence.

The Dawn of Understanding

He was no longer the young, inexperienced fox who had set out on a journey of discovery. He was now a bearer of wisdom, a carrier of the legacy that had been passed down through the ages. And he knew that he would carry that legacy with pride, with honor, with the strength that came from knowing he was part of something timeless that would endure long after he was gone.

As the sun continued to rise, casting its light over the world, Finn took his first step forward, his heart filled with the dawn of understanding. He was ready to face the challenges of the future, ready to continue his journey with patience, wisdom, and the quiet strength that had been forged in the fires of his trials.

And as he walked, the Great Willow's whispers echoed softly in his mind, a reminder that he was never alone, that the wisdom of the ages would always be with him, guiding him, supporting him, helping him to grow into the leader, guide, and bearer of wisdom that he was destined to become.

The dawn of understanding had broken, and with it, a new chapter in Finn's journey had begun. It was to be a chapter filled with hope, promise, and the quiet certainty that whatever lay ahead, he would face it with the strength and wisdom that had brought him this far.

And as the first light of day bathed the world in its golden glow, Finn knew that he was ready to walk the path of wisdom, patience, and understanding, carrying the legacy of Everleaf with him wherever his journey might lead.

A Page from Finn's Journal

"The Slow Path"

I used to fear the slow path—
the one where nothing seems to happen,
where silence is your only companion.

But now I see—it's not empty.
The slowness holds meaning
the fast cannot carry.

It's in the pauses between thoughts,
the breath before a truth is spoken.

Wisdom doesn't arrive with thunder.
It walks like the Tortoise—
sure-footed, timeless, and patient.

I walk slower now.
But I hear more.

Finn

The Echo of Time

The forest of Everleaf was bathed in the soft, golden light of late afternoon. The air was warm and still, carrying with it the scent of earth and foliage, a reminder of the eternal cycles that governed the world. It was a scene of quiet beauty, a place where time seemed to slow down, where the rush of the outside world faded into a distant memory.

Finn stood at the edge of a small clearing, his eyes taking in the familiar surroundings with a sense of calm that came from deep within. The journey he had undertaken, the lessons he had learned, had brought him to this moment—a moment of reflection, of peace, of understanding. He had returned to Everleaf, but he was not the same fox who had set out on his journey. He was now a bearer of wisdom, a guide for those who would one day walk the same path.

The Tortoise's Timeless Wisdom

As he looked around the clearing, Finn noticed a group of young animals gathered nearby, their eyes wide with curiosity as they listened to an elder squirrel recount a story from the past. The squirrel's voice was soft but firm, carrying the weight of experience, the lessons of time. Finn smiled, recognizing in the squirrel's words the same wisdom that Griselda had imparted to him, the same understanding of patience; of time; of the slow, deliberate unfolding of life's mysteries.

As he approached the group, his presence was met with warm smiles and respectful nods. The young ones looked up at him with a mixture of awe and admiration, their eyes shining with the eagerness of those who had yet to face the challenges of the world. Finn could see in them a reflection of his own younger self, the same hunger for knowledge, the same desire to understand the world around them.

One of the young foxes, a small, sprightly creature with bright eyes and a bushy tail, stepped forward, his voice filled with excitement. "Finn, is it true that you faced the darkness and learned the secrets of time? Is it true that you can hear the whispers of the Great Willow?"

Finn crouched down to meet the young fox's gaze, his smile gentle. "Yes, it's true," he replied, his voice calm and reassuring. "But the wisdom I've gained is not just about hearing the whispers or facing the darkness. It's about learning to listen, be patient, and trust in the rhythm of the world around us. It's about understanding that wisdom is not something we conquer, but something we grow into, slowly, over time."

The Echo of Time

The young fox's eyes widened, his curiosity piqued. "Can you teach us, Finn? Can you help us learn the wisdom of Everleaf?"

Finn felt a warmth in his chest, a sense of fulfillment that came from knowing that the knowledge he had gained would not end with him but would continue to grow, to spread, to guide others. He nodded, his expression serious but kind. "Of course. But remember, learning wisdom is a journey, not a destination. It takes time, patience, and a willingness to listen to the world around you, the voices of those who came before you, and the quiet whisper of your own heart."

As the young ones gathered closer, eager to hear more, Finn began to speak, sharing with them the stories of his journey, the lessons he had learned from Griselda, the trials he had faced, and the understanding he had gained. His words flowed like the gentle breeze that rustled through the trees, carrying with them the essence of the wisdom he had cultivated, the patience that had become a part of him.

And as he spoke, he felt Griselda's presence, not as a physical being but as a legacy that lived on in the forest, in the very fabric of Everleaf. Her wisdom was woven into the roots of the trees, into the whispers of the wind, into the cycles of time that governed the world. She was no longer by his side, guiding him with her steady voice, but her influence remained, a constant, enduring presence that would continue to shape the lives of those who sought to understand the deeper truths of the world.

The Tortoise's Timeless Wisdom

The sun dipped lower in the sky, casting a warm, amber glow over the clearing. The young ones listened intently, their eyes filled with wonder, their minds absorbing the lessons that Finn imparted. It was a moment of connection—of continuity, a passing of the torch from one generation to the next, from one seeker of wisdom to those who would one day walk the same path.

As the day drew to a close, the young ones began to drift away, their hearts and minds filled with the stories they had heard, the wisdom they had begun to grasp. Finn watched them go, a sense of quiet satisfaction settling over him. He had done his part, but he knew that his journey was far from over. There were still challenges to face, lessons to learn, and wisdom to pass on.

The shadows lengthened, and Finn turned his gaze toward the horizon, where the first stars were beginning to appear in the darkening sky. The world was vast, filled with mysteries that he had yet to explore, but he felt no fear, no hesitation. He was ready to face whatever came next, armed with the timeless wisdom he had gained, the patience that had become his greatest strength.

The Great Willow's whispers echoed faintly in his mind, a reminder that time was not just a measure of days and years, but a force that shaped the very fabric of existence. It was a force that he had learned to trust and to move with rather than against—a force to guide him through the uncertainties of life.

And as he stood there, the echo of time resonating in his heart, Finn knew that he was not alone. He was part of

something greater, something timeless, something that connected him to the past, the present, and the future. He was a bearer of wisdom, a guide for those who would come after him, a link in the unbroken chain of knowledge that stretched across the ages.

The darkness still lingered on the edges of the world, a reminder that the challenges were not over, that there were still battles to be fought, still mysteries to be unraveled. But Finn was no longer the young, uncertain fox who had set out on a journey of discovery. He was now a creature of patience, of understanding, of quiet strength.

He took a deep breath of cool night air and turned away from the horizon. There was still work to be done, wisdom to be shared, and paths to be walked. And as he began to make his way back into the heart of Everleaf, Finn felt a deep sense of peace, of readiness, of quiet determination.

The journey would never be over, but with each step, Finn knew that he was walking the path of wisdom and time that would lead him to whatever lay ahead. And he knew, with a certainty that resonated deep within his soul, that he was ready to face the future, to embrace the challenges, to continue the journey with the strength and wisdom that had been passed down through the ages.

The echo of time would continue to guide him, shape him, and help him grow. And as the first light of a new day began to break over the horizon, Finn knew that he was prepared to face whatever came next, with the wisdom of the past, the strength of the present, and the hope of the future as his constant companions.

The Tortoise's Timeless Wisdom

The dawn of understanding had brought him to this moment, and with it, the promise of a journey that would continue to unfold—a journey that would lead him to new heights, new depths, new horizons. And with that promise in his heart, Finn walked forward, ready to embrace the future and carry the echo of time with him wherever his journey might lead.

The Rune of Time

The hush of Everleaf deepened. Even after the murmurs of the forest had stilled, and the last echoes of the Council faded into the stillness of night, Finn remained alone, yet entirely not. A weight hung in the branches above him, not of fear, but of becoming.

He sat beneath the ancient willow again, the very place where his journey began in whispers and winds. It was here that the leaves once danced with riddles, and the roots had sighed truths too old for the tongue. How young he had been then. How impossibly small. Now, he could feel it, the stirrings of something vast…something watching.

He closed his eyes and remembered the tortoise's voice, slow and patient like time itself:

"The deepest truths do not rush. They wait for you to earn them."

And hadn't he earned something? The bruises on his heart said yes. But wisdom, it seemed, only widened the unknown.

Tonight, the stars burned differently, more focused, more ancient. The constellations seemed to shift subtly into an unfamiliar shape. One that looked like—

Finn blinked. A glow pulsed beneath his palm.

There, etched into the bark beneath his fingers, was a mark he had never noticed before: a rune. Spiraled, radiant, vibrating faintly with energy that felt both new and impossibly old.

The Rune of Time.

A whisper moved through the leaves.

"Not all who wander are called. But you, Finn, are being summoned..."

Summoned?

By whom?

For what?

He felt a tug—not physical, but spiritual—as if something from beyond the veil of time was beckoning. Not forward, but deeper.

The Rune of Time

And then, just for a heartbeat, he heard it—a child's laughter. His laughter. The memory of his first moment under the willow tree, asking if trees could speak.

He opened his eyes to silence.

Had he imagined it?

No. He knew the signs now. The awakening wasn't over. It had only just begun.

Something was approaching. Something elemental. Not evil, perhaps, but dangerous. And he would not face it as a child.

He would face it as something else entirely.

The rune pulsed again, brighter this time.

"Time," the wind seemed to say, "is no longer a river. It is a choice."

Finn rose slowly, every part of him buzzing with a question that had no shape but demanded an answer.

Somewhere beyond the forest, the next path waited.

And the Rune of Time burned.

*What is the whisper that echoes
through the leaves of Everleaf?*

Who marked the Rune of Time?

*Why does Finn feel the journey
has only just begun?*

Book 3 is coming...

And it knows your name.

Enjoy this exclusive sneak peek from the next
installment of Whispers of the Willow

THE CROW'S TEMPTING KNOWLEDGE

✳ ·········· Book Three ·········· ✳

Whispers of the Willow:
The Chronicles of Finn and the Hidden Truth

Chapter 1

The Mysterious Encounter

The light of the day began to wane as Finn ventured deeper into the forest, the shadows lengthening with every step. Everleaf, usually so alive with the songs of birds and the rustle of leaves, had grown eerily quiet. The silence was unsettling, pressing in on him like a tangible force, making him acutely aware of each breath, each footfall on the soft, mossy ground.

Finn's instincts were on high alert. He had walked these paths many times before, yet now they seemed unfamiliar, shrouded in a darkness that went beyond the simple absence of light. The trees loomed taller, their branches twisted and gnarled, as if the forest itself were holding its breath, waiting for something to happen.

The Crow's Tempting Knowledge

As he moved forward, Finn felt a strange pull, a magnetic force drawing him deeper into the heart of the woods. It was as if the forest was guiding him toward something— or someone. The whispers of the Great Willow had hinted at a test, a challenge that would force him to confront the very essence of knowledge and wisdom. But there had been no mention of this oppressive silence, this sense of foreboding that now wrapped itself around him like a suffocating cloak.

Suddenly, Finn stopped in his tracks. There, just ahead, in a small clearing where the last rays of sunlight barely penetrated, sat a figure. A crow, perched on a low-hanging branch. Its feathers were as black as midnight. The bird's eyes, sharp and gleaming, locked onto Finn with an intensity that sent a shiver down his spine.

The crow seemed to belong to the darkness, an extension of the shadows that surrounded it. Its presence was both unsettling and mesmerizing, a paradox that made Finn's heart race with a mix of fear and curiosity. He had heard tales of crows—birds of mystery, harbingers of change, creatures who danced on the fine line between knowledge and deception. But he had never encountered one like this, so tangible, so present, so undeniably real.

"Welcome, young seeker," the crow croaked, its voice low and gravelly, yet strangely melodic. "I have been waiting for you."

The Mysterious Encounter

Finn's breath caught in his throat. The bird spoke with a familiarity that unnerved him, as if it had known him all along, had watched his every step, had anticipated this very moment.

"Who are you?" Finn asked, his voice barely above a whisper.

The crow tilted its head, a gleam of amusement flickering in its dark eyes. "Names are but shadows, fleeting and inconsequential. What matters is the knowledge I can offer you, the answers to the questions that burn within you."

Finn felt a pull, an almost irresistible urge to step closer, to hear more. The crow's words were like honey, sweet and alluring, promising the satisfaction of curiosity, the fulfillment of understanding. But beneath that sweetness, Finn sensed something else—a bitterness, a warning that something was not quite right.

"What kind of knowledge?" Finn asked cautiously, his eyes narrowing as he studied the bird. The crow's beak curved into what might have been a smile, though on a crow's face, it was difficult to tell.

"The kind that reveals the hidden truths of this world, the kind that answers the deepest questions of your heart. I can show you the secrets that lie within the shadows, the knowledge that others fear to uncover."

The Crow's Tempting Knowledge

The offer was tempting, almost too tempting. Finn's mind raced with possibilities, with the allure of finally understanding the mysteries that had eluded him for so long. But something held him back, a quiet voice within that whispered of the dangers of easy answers, of knowledge that came without the effort of seeking it out.

"How do I know I can trust you?" Finn asked, his voice steady despite the unease that gnawed at him.

The crow let out a soft, mocking laugh, a sound that sent a chill down Finn's spine. "Trust is a fragile thing, young one. It is given too freely by some, too sparingly by others. But knowledge—knowledge is eternal, unchanging. It does not require trust, only acceptance."

Finn felt a surge of doubt, a pang of uncertainty that cut through the allure of the crow's words. There was something in the bird's tone, in the way it spoke of knowledge as if it were a commodity to be traded, that made Finn's fur bristle with unease.

"What's the cost?" Finn asked, his eyes narrowing as he tried to see past the crow's enigmatic facade.

The crow's eyes gleamed with a predatory light, its voice dropping to a whisper. "The cost? There is always a cost, young fox. But that is for you to decide. Will you pay the price for easy answers, for knowledge that comes without the burden of seeking? Or will you choose the harder path, the one that requires effort, patience, and the willingness to question even the answers you find?"

Finn's heart pounded in his chest, the weight of the decision pressing down on him like a heavy stone. The crow's offer was tantalizing; it held the promise of knowledge without struggle, of answers without doubt. But Finn knew that the easiest path was rarely the right one. The lessons he had learned from Griselda and the wisdom of the Great Willow pointed to the value of patience, of seeking understanding through experience rather than shortcuts.

"I will not be tempted by easy answers," Finn said firmly, taking a step back from the crow. "I seek true wisdom, not just knowledge. I will find my own way."

The crow's eyes flashed with something like anger, or perhaps disappointment, though its expression remained inscrutable. "Very well, young seeker," it said, its voice now colder, more distant. "But remember, the path you choose is fraught with uncertainty, with trials that will test not just your strength but your very understanding of the world. Do not think that true wisdom comes easily or without cost."

With that, the crow spread its wings and took flight, disappearing into the shadows of the forest as quickly as it had appeared. Finn watched it go, his heart still racing,

his mind swirling with thoughts. The encounter had left him shaken but also resolute. He knew now that the path to true wisdom was lined with temptations and pitfalls that could easily lead him astray.

But Finn was determined. He would not be swayed by the promise of quick knowledge or easy answers. He would seek the deeper truths, the wisdom that could only be gained through patience, reflection, and the courage to question even the most alluring of truths.

As the last light of day faded and the forest was plunged into darkness, Finn felt a renewed sense of purpose. The journey ahead would be difficult, but he was ready. The encounter with the crow had shown him the dangers that lay in wait, but it had also strengthened his resolve.

He turned away from the clearing, his eyes fixed on the path ahead. The forest was vast, and there was much to learn, much to discover. But Finn knew that with the guidance of the Great Willow and the lessons he had already learned, he would find his way. The allure of the unknown was strong, but Finn's resolve was stronger. And with that knowledge, he began to walk, his steps sure, his heart filled with the quiet determination to seek true wisdom, no matter the cost.

Dear Explorer of Everleaf:

If you are reading this, you have walked with Finn farther than most. You have felt the quiet wisdom of the tortoise, heard the crow's ancient riddles, and stood at the edge of what cannot yet be named. That means something.

It means you are not just reading a story. You are part of a journey.

The Chronicles of Finn and the Hidden Truth were never meant to be read in passing. They are meant to unfold — slowly, meaningfully, deeply — just as wisdom does.

Book by book.

Rune by rune.

Leaf by leaf.

As we move into Book 3, and then onward to Book 12, I ask only this:

Stay.

Stay with Finn as he grows. Stay with the whispers in the forest. Stay with the questions that do not have answers yet.

Because this world we are building — you and I — is made not of ink and paper alone.

It is made of belief.

Of imagination.

Of readers who choose to journey rather than skip ahead.

If Book 1 awakened something in you, and Book 2 deepened it, then what comes next will change you.

We are only just beginning.

With all my wonder and gratitude.

Anthony Ofili Nwosisi

Author of The Chronicles of Finn and the Hidden Truth

Anthony Ofili Nwosisi is a scholar, storyteller, and architect of insight who writes at the edge where artificial intelligence confronts human complexity. As a doctoral researcher in Explainable AI (XAI) at the University of Amsterdam, he explores how intelligent systems reshape creativity, redefine failure, and alter the pathways of organizational learning and innovation. His academic work probes not only how machines process data—but how humans adapt, err, and evolve when those machines become decision-makers. His focus is clarity in complexity. Truth amidst opacity.

But Anthony's voice does not stop at research. It resounds through narrative.

He is the visionary behind *Whispers of the Willow: The Chronicles of Finn and the Hidden Truth*—a profound twelve-book saga that weaves timeless virtues into the pulse of an enchanted, yet deeply human world. These are not children's books, nor are they merely fantastical tales. They are carefully layered odysseys that teach resilience, awaken moral courage, and guide the reader—young or old—through the hidden architecture of wisdom.

Whether decoding the neural scaffolding of AI systems or constructing allegorical universes where characters face the agony of choice and the burden of knowledge, Anthony's work is unified by one pursuit: ***to awaken discernment in an age numbed by automation.***

He does not separate science from story, nor mind from soul. He writes to reconcile them.

To pierce the fog. To restore memory. To illuminate truth.